THE GHOSTS OF GADUS ISLAND

ALSO BY DAVID H. ROPER

Watching for Mermaids
Beyond Mermaids…Life's Tangles, Knots and Bends
Rounding the Bend
Getting the Job You Want…Now!

THE GHOSTS OF GADUS ISLAND

A Story of Young Love, Loss,
and the Order of Nature

DAVID H. ROPER

Best-selling author of
Watching For Mermaids

Points East Publishing, Inc.

Published by: Points East Publishing, Inc.

Cover and Interior Design: Creative Publishing Book Design

ISBN Paperback: 978-0-9856501-9-3

For Mary Kay

Sometimes the hero stumbles
and falls right off the page.
Sometimes the princess
rolls her eyes and says,
"I don't want to be saved."
Sometimes the dragon needs rescuing
and the villain aches to be helped.
Sometimes, in the darkness,
the lost boy finds himself.
Sometimes the prince is cunning
and not at all who he seemed.
Sometimes the witch's kindness shows
it's she who deserves to be queen.
Sometimes we shouldn't define people
based on somebody else's point of view -
just because it's what we've been told
Doesn't make it true.

      "Sometimes the Wolf Cries Girl" - srwpoetry

Life will break you. Nobody can protect you from that, and living alone won't either, for solitude will also break you with its yearning. You have to love. You have to feel. It is the reason you are here on earth. You are here to risk your heart.

— Louise Erdrich, *The Painted Drum*

Table of Contents

I

August 11, 1967 – Morning, Day 1
A Remote Island Off the Coast of Maine

A tall teenaged girl moves close to the cliff's edge, looks out to sea, runs her hands through her hair. She's wearing cutoff shorts; hung from the back pockets are rose hips and fiddlehead ferns. She's hot and winded from the climb. Anxious about her surroundings. Cautiously, she backs away from the cliff edge, glancing behind her at a grouping of spruce, as if expecting someone or something to jump out at her. There's a shattering sound like the breaking of glass. She moves carefully back toward the edge of the cliff. She looks below. It's that boy! He's there! She backs away quickly to the middle of the clearing. Turns in a small circle while rubbing her hands together. What to do? She's filled with uncertainty. Should she go back? Yell down? But then what? She inches back to the cliff edge and peers below. He appears to be speaking to someone, but she sees no one else, hears no response. He's holding a green bottle in one hand and a short piece of stick in the other as he walks along the stone beach toward one of the high sides of the cliff that borders the cove. He places the green bottle on a crude table of driftwood slats laid across two large rocks at the base of the cliff. More driftwood boards lean against the ledge behind the table. A spear, like a javelin, only thinner, is imbedded in one of them. He bends down and pulls it out of the board, looks up, and seems to speak in the direction of a few scraggly spruce a few feet up the cliff behind the target. She can't hear what he's saying. Then he nods, as if receiving guidance or instruction, before he returns to the spot where she'd first spied on him. Facing the new bottle on the flat rock, which is about thirty paces away, he clasps the short stick and the long, thin spear together over his head, puts a foot forward and leans back. He's like a baseball pitcher in windup, his throwing hand holding the spear above and behind his head now, and then, with a grunt and a great snap of his wrist, he throws the spear, the shorter stick somehow catapulting the feathered end of the spear even faster at the final arc of his throw, distorting its shape as it sails through the air toward its target. The green bottle shatters: the spear passes through it and sticks in the driftwood board behind. She is amazed. Before she realizes it, she begins clapping. The boy looks up. Stares at her. She stares back. Frozen.

"You should not be here. You should not stay on this island. Go," he says, forcefully.

"I…I just wanted to say, 'thank you'. For today, I mean. For pulling us off the ledge."

"Go."

She backs away a bit, but stays in sight of the boy. She gives a smile. "Well, you're sure a good shot," she says, nodding. "What you're using there, is that some kind of—"

"Go!" he yells, then moves to pick up his spear before turning and heading away from her, down the beach, moving in the quick, surefooted manner of a creature in its natural habitat. She watches, not sure if she feels hurt or scared by his reaction to her. He turns to the cliff at the end of the beach and begins to climb quickly, holding his long spear in one hand, moving like a mountain goat up a rough trail through a steep, jagged area of cliff, having foregone the easier path back near the girl. She continues to watch him, sees him glance back at her, then drops from sight. He doesn't reappear. She turns away from her perch to go. There's a cry. She turns back. He's there now, half standing. Something's wrong. "Are you alright?" she yells. He doesn't respond. She yells again. No response. "I'll go get help," she says.

"No. Just you. You help. Come. Down to the beach."

Carefully, the girl works her way down the steep path to the beach, then hurries as best she can through the popplestones, her ankles twisting as her sneakers slide off each large round stone. The boy is on his side, lying about twenty feet up the rough, steep trail; he's holding his foot, wincing. To the girl, he's a strange sight, like a wounded animal covered in dirt. Small stones and sticks cling to the front of his grey sweatshirt. There's a small leafy twig stuck in his long black hair, and most of the small bones and beads on the cord around his neck now hang over his shoulder. She moves cautiously to a few feet below him, looks up at him, uncertain, a bit fearful of being so close. He looks back. She's startled by his eyes. One is dark brown; the other is a bright emerald green, like the eye of her friend Moira's husky. This boy's eyes are watchful, wary, but also striking, inquisitive, with startling clarity. He moans.

"Is it your ankle?"

"Yes."

"What…what should I do?"

"The cabin. Help me to the cabin." He gestures to a spot above.

"There? How? It's so—"

"You're tall. Strong. You can help me up. I'll be fine in the cabin. Then you will go."

She moves closer. Puts out a hand. The boy grabs her wrist, props himself up on one knee, then strains to rise. One of his feet slips a bit, causing several stones to slide down the path. She feels tension on her wrist as he pulls on her arm to stop his slide. It's too precarious for the girl. "I don't think this—"

"No. I will stand. Just hold my wrist."

"But why don't I go get help?"

It's as if that question is the impetus he needs to stand. He winces again. Steadies himself. Stares at her. "I'll need to put my arm over your shoulder," he says. She's frightened. Afraid of some sudden or strange reaction from him. But before she can react, he's put his arm around her. From his closeness comes the smell of sweat, but there's also something else: it's the scent of the land—trees, resin, moss, bark, and pinecones—they all seem to be a part of him. The touch of their bodies is tentative; they're both on edge. The girl thinks of the wild stallion she had watched in the Tucson corral that winter; the saddle just on, but not cinched; the wrangler bending down, an arm stroking the horse's flank, the other arm slowly reaching to tighten the saddle; the wariness in the large, clear, watchful eye of the horse; and the feeling that a sudden, violent reaction is imminent.

As they slowly hobble up the path, carefully navigating the twisted roots strewn between the rocks, the girl wonders: what is this strange boy thinking? What is he feeling? Has he ever even touched a girl? Is he crazy? If so, what could, what would, he do to her? Her fear returns for a moment, until she thinks: no, he couldn't do much to her, not with that sprained ankle of his. She concentrates on her footing, and on looking ahead, up the trail, but not at the boy. She feels him tense up with each stab of pain, but she senses he is also trying his hardest to stifle his hurt, as if to avoid any sympathy. The trail angles to the right now. Begins to flatten out. And there! A small, weathered, rough shingled cabin. Or half a cabin, she thinks, chopped off in the middle, as if the builder just ran out of time or lumber, or didn't want to bother to cut down the tall spruce trees where the other half of the cabin could be situated. There are three small wooden steps leading to an unpainted screen door on the right. Hanging next to the door is a tattered flag made up of four squares, two yellow and two black. On the left side of the cabin is a window, half open. Above it the steeply slanted roof rises to the peak and abruptly stops, leaving a straight, flat, unwindowed wall for the other half of the cabin. It reminds the girl of those half sections of mobile homes she's seen being trucked down the highway.

"This is good," the boy says. "You can leave me here. I can hop the rest of the way." He begins to remove his arm from around her shoulder. Tries to hop. But the hopping motion is too jarring on his bad ankle. For the first time he screams out, then wobbles. She quickly moves back to him. Takes his arm. He pulls it away and puts it back around her shoulder. "All right. A little farther, I guess." They move slowly to the steps under the narrow screen door, then hesitate, both trying to plan the next move. The door is too narrow for both of them to move through at once, and making three hopping steps with one foot will cause him more pain. She senses they both realize this. "I should sit for a moment. Sit and think," he says. She helps lower him to the top step. The boy is quiet for an uncomfortably long time. Finally, to break the silence, she asks, "What's that flag mean, anyway?"

"It's the Q flag. The isolation flag. For quarantine."

For the first time, the girl smiles and shakes her head. "Quarantine? Isolation? Now that's the *last* thing we need right now!" She hopes he'll smile back. Instead, he just stares at her and shakes his head, straight faced.

"Well, look, if I go in first, I can get behind you and lift you, back first" she says. "Under your arms. Take the pressure off that foot. You can gently step up each step with your bad foot just as I lift you up to take the weight off."

The boy nods. She moves by him into the cabin. Props the door open with a brick she finds on the floor. Looks around. It's one room. There's a rough pine floor. Some of the furnishings, a spindle bed, along with two chairs, appear rustic and handmade from small logs, saplings and driftwood. Two stacked lobster traps, with an old piece of plywood serve as a table by the chairs. On it is a kerosene lamp, its mantle clouded with soot. A thick, hardcover book sits open next to the lamp. She sees a rusted green metal camp stove on a turquoise Formica kitchen table supported by three metal legs and a 2x4 wooden replacement which serves as the fourth. Under the table, between two vinyl-backed chairs, she spies a dented Coleman cooler. In the middle of the cabin a black cast iron wood stove with its dented aluminum chimney faces her like a silent sentry. But the girl is most surprised by what is on the opposite wall of the cabin. Along its full length are crude wooden shelves filled with books. Hundreds of books.

"Now we can try," he says.

It works. She gets him up the steps and through the door. She continues backing up with him, lifting under his arms while he tentatively follows. "Where now?" she asks, looking at one of the chairs and then over her shoulder at the bed.

"The bed," he says, and slowly they move to it.

She helps him down. He sits and then leans forward. Puts his head in his hands. She moves back a few steps. She's nervous now, thinking about what she'd said about quarantine, how she'd underscored the fact that the two of them are truly isolated here. He knows that, of course. Her mind flashes on him throwing that spear on the beach. The violence of it. The bottle shattering. But then it dawns on her that she's completely safe from him as long as she stays out of his reach. He can't run after her. He can't even walk. And he *has* been tentative with her. It all gives her the courage to push a bit, ask some questions. "Maybe I should find your parents?" He lifts his head from his hands. Stares at her. No, it's not *at* her; it's an unfocused, detached stare that goes right through her, out the screen door and way beyond. She thinks of the cover of *Life Magazine* she'd seen that winter, with the picture of a shell-shocked Marine in Vietnam, a young man with a look the magazine cover called "the thousand-yard stare". Something's very wrong with this boy, she thinks. "Or look," she continues, "I'll just go get *someone*. Someone to help."

"No," he says, finally. "You need to go. Now!"

"I can't just leave you here," she says.

"It's my prerogative. My cabin. You're being intrusive."

His use of big words surprises her. She looks up at the rows of books. "These are your books, aren't they?"

He nods.

"I bet you read a lot. Me, too." She sees a glimmer of interest in his eyes.

"You need to go."

She feels rebuffed. "Well, if no one is coming to check on you, I'll have to come back."

"It will heal."

"That will take days. What about food? Water?"

"It's here. There's enough. I will hop to it. And I have helpers."

The girl is perplexed. "Your parents?"

The boy doesn't respond.

"Because it doesn't seem like there's anyone else on this island"

"There are lots of them."

"Them?"

No answer.

"So, you don't want me to come back?" the girl says, finally.

The boy looks away. Says nothing.

She turns to go. As she grabs the crude wooden handle of the screen door, her back to him, she hesitates, somehow sensing that he may say something. He does.

"What I do want is that you tell no one about me being hurt, including that old man on your boat."

She turns to him. "That's my grandfather."

"Do not tell him anything about me. You must promise." He shook his head. "You should never have sailed so close to our ledges. None of this would have happened. You would not be here now. You could have sailed past farther offshore to wherever you were going in the first place."

"We were going here."

"No. No one goes to Gadus Island. It's not for others."

"Why? Is it private?"

"You should not be here."

His commanding tone emboldens her. "Well, sorry, but I'm here now." She holds out her hand. "Anyway, my name's Cleo. And you are?"

The boy only stares back at her. She gets an idea. "You know, my Poppy—that's what I call him…my grandfather I mean—well, he's an archeologist and kind of an expert on the Red Paint People, and that's why we're here. And, well, the way I bet you know every inch of this island and all, you could help him once your foot is better. And if his theories are correct, you could be a part of some amazing archeological discoveries."

The boy's behavior suddenly becomes more bizarre; he frantically fingers the bones and beads on the cord around his neck; his eyes dart past the girl to an empty corner of the cabin. He nods urgently, vigorously, at something, or at nothing. Then he starts padding the air, as if pushing someone or something back.

It's all too much for the girl; she's down the three steps of the cabin and in a full run before the screen door bangs shut.

II

18 Years Later – July 7, 1985
The Sloop *Archaic*, Nine Miles East
of Gadus Island

I t had gotten cool, and the wind began to increase and turn north-east. This gave Cleo concern. She locked the wheel for a moment and leaned forward to winch in the jib a bit, glancing below decks at Sophie, who was still sitting at the navigation table, still in her shorts and bathing suit top, and still writing feverishly in her diary.

They were working their way up the coast of Maine from Massachusetts aboard *Archaic*, the old wooden sloop which Poppy, Cleo's archeologist grandfather, had passed down to her the year before.

The wind continued to build. Cleo began to worry about *Archaic*, and this drove her thoughts back to her conversation with her grandfather that last day in Salem Hospital that winter, while she held his frail but still warm hand.

He'd lifted his oxygen mask, taken a deep, raspy breath, as if to gather one last round of strength. "The boat's yours now, so take care of her; don't push her too hard to windward in a stiff breeze," he'd said. Then he'd paused, closing his eyes for so long that Cleo thought the worst. Then they opened, focused back on his granddaughter. "It's kind of like life, isn't it; to know when not to push too hard; to keep balance. Otherwise, things can go awry."

"I'll sail her the way you taught me, Poppy. Always." Cleo paused, turning her head away, trying to stifle a sob. "But it won't be the same," she continued, patting the top of his hand.

Poppy said something Cleo couldn't quite make out, so she leaned closer and gave him a quizzical half smile. "Did you say 'chainplates', Poppy?"

"They hold the mast up, dear. You know; they fasten the shrouds to the hull. They're old, weak. Check them out, okay? And the mast. The mast is old. And those garboard planks down next to the keel, well, if they open up in a rough sea…"

"I'll check everything out. I promise. Maybe when you get out of here, together we can…"

Poppy had interrupted, shaking his head. "No. It's time to let go, sweet Ohkuk," he said, using the nickname he'd given her when she was a child. He'd smiled, as if about to make one last joke in his life. "My chainplates are rusted out. My mast will fall down soon. And when I'm gone, well, ha!… no one will have to dig up the bones of this old archeologist, because we know *his* story, don't we, Ohkuk."

Cleo nodded. Poppy was quiet for a bit before continuing. "But it's been a great sail. For both of us, I daresay. So, you keep *Archaic* going as long as you can. Keep exploring. Do it with your own young girl. Show her…"

Poppy had closed his eyes then, and Cleo backed out quietly from the room. But halfway down the hospital hallway she remembered her gloves, and returned, carefully, noiselessly, opening his door and tiptoeing in. As she was backing out again, gloves in hand, he spoke, now wide eyed, startling her: "Way back. That young island boy on Gadus. Remember? Back when you were a teenager. Well, I saw him. And a fish. A big fish. In a dream. But the boy was now a grown man…and he was struggling…struggling to find the surface from under a big dark sea."

* * *

And now months later, Poppy gone, and miles out at sea, here she was even more worried about *Archaic*. Cleo locked the wheel again and leaned down the hatch. "Sophie, I'm not liking this wind shift; and it's starting to get rough." She gave a worried look at the darkening horizon and building seas. "I want to make a safe harbor farther east, but the wind is bucking us; we may have to fall off and

13

head…somewhere else." Cleo knew all too well that there was only one 'somewhere else' to be reached before dark, and that was an island with numerous sunken ledges guarding its tiny slit of a harbor, an island that had haunted her memory for many years.

She looked down the hatch. "Sophie, did you hear me?" Sophie didn't look up. "Whatever, Mom," came her only acknowledgement. Cleo zipped up her sweatshirt and shook her head. There had been so many eyerolls and 'whatever's' from Sophie since, and even before they'd left. Cleo had thought this trip would be good for her, giving her some space from whatever messiness was swirling around in that seventeen-year-old brain of hers. Maybe they could finally talk things out on the boat, she'd thought, in a place where there were no distractions, where there could be no 'I'm going out for a while' from her daughter. So, before they'd left, Cleo had talked up the trip whenever she found a window when Sophie might be listening. She had told her about the island exploring she and her grandfather had done, about the challenges and rewards of finding their way in the fog, navigating by using all their senses. About whales breeching and about those seemingly smiling seals playfully romping around the old skiff while she and Poppy rowed ashore in hopes of finding clues and perhaps even discovering relics of some ancient world.

Was she naïve about all this, Cleo thought, naïve about believing a teenage girl of today would want to live on a boat for a month with her mother, away from all her shore life? Just because she had always been adventurous, was that any reason to make Sophie that way? Was it all so different today from when she was Sophie's age? And that made her think of Aiden, until, out of nowhere, a nasty cross sea emerged and shook *Archaic*, spray flying over the cockpit coaming and drenching Cleo. "That's it," she yelled, half to herself and half down to Sophie. "We're falling off, going downwind; it's only going to get worse." And with that she turned the wheel, eased the mainsheet, set a new course in the approximate direction, locked the wheel for a moment, and slacked the jib. *Archaic* and their floating world stopped bucking in the now following seas, and her hull speed increased with the wind astern. Cleo still had to navigate, though, and she had to go below decks to do it. She put some urgency in her tone: "Sophie, you need to come up on deck right *now* and take the wheel while I plot a new course."

When Sophie finally did appear, wrestling with the zipper on her orange foul weather jacket, Cleo pointed at *Archaic's* old binnacle. "Just steer this course; between 320 and 340 degrees is close enough for now." Sophie grabbed the cockpit coaming, then looked aft at the large following seas. "Mom, I'm not sure I can…"

"Just try, sweetie; you can do it. I trust you. Now get behind the wheel."

"Okay, okay. But don't read my diary when you're down there…"

"God, Sophie, that's the last thing on my mind right now. We need to try to make this island's entrance and get in before dark so we can see our way past the ledges; there's ledges with breaking seas everywhere at the entrance. So just steer the course, okay?"

"Okay. You said that, Mom."

"Sophie, just steer the course! This is serious!"

Sophie started to sob. "Mom, I want to go back. Home. Why did you bring me out here?"

"Okay, look. Please, just steer and when we get in, we'll discuss it when we're safely anchored in the harbor."

"What harbor? What island? I don't see anything anywhere."

"You can't see it yet, it's about nine or ten miles ahead."

15

And with that Cleo headed down the cabin steps to lay the exact course. *Archaic's* rolling had rearranged much of the contents of the cabin, and Cleo picked up and dumped random things into the deep galley sink as she passed: a bunch of bananas, an orange, a water bottle, a bag of cookies. She tossed Sophie's diary onto the starboard bunk, slid in behind the varnished mahogany navigation desk, lifted the cover, pulled out and unfolded the chart they'd been using, grabbed the parallel rules and divider tools, and began to plot the new course. It would not be perfect, as she didn't know her exact current location to plot from, and the now heavy rolling motion of *Archaic* caused by the building seas and Sophie's erratic steering made it hard to hold the plotting tools in place. Still, after triple checking her figures, she headed up on deck, and took the wheel from Sophie.

"Good job. It's 330 degrees and about nine miles away," she said, wiping some spray from the compass glass. She glanced at Sophie; the color had gone from her face; her raven black hair was matted to her forehead, and she was shivering. "Sophie, sweetie, just look at the horizon; don't go back into the cabin; you'll get seasick down there. We'll be in before you know it. Hey, let's see who can be the first to spot the island. It won't be long. We must be doing six, maybe seven knots."

Sophie sat silently in the cockpit, staring forward, a frozen look on her face, her knuckles white as she gripped the salt-stained cockpit coaming each time *Archaic* slid down the larger seas.

Cleo was a good sailor. A damn good sailor. She had learned from a master; and she knew what her grandfather Poppy would have said: most ship disasters happen because of land, not the deep blue sea; the land is your enemy in a storm or in darkness or when you're uncertain of your location. It's hard to do, but your best recourse then is to head straight out to sea and wait it out; wait for the winds to subside; wait for daylight; wait until through some means you can truly identify your position—then go back to the land. Deep down Cleo knew that's what she should do now. But it's hard to adhere to practical advice when your mind can't stop thinking of a quiet harbor, a warm dry cabin, or, in this case, a teenager already on the edge for other reasons. No, she was going to try to make it in, and because of this she would have to take one more trip below to review the entrance directions on the old cruising guide on the shelf by the navigation desk. At that point Sophie would have to take the wheel again. There was no choice. In the meantime, Cleo continued to steer, trying to maintain a steady course down the rolling seas, while looking ahead in search of the island. After about an hour, Sophie gamely took the wheel and Cleo headed below.

The old, mildewed cruising guide still held her grandfather's notes, written in his precise, clean penmanship underneath the printed entry instructions the guide provided, which read:

Lying just under the slate gray surface of the sea, as if poised for attack, large undersea ledges guard the small harbor entrance to what appears to be an unremarkable island, a two-mile long sliver of land that seems suspended in time, its marshes, moors, and bayberry-crowded trails traversed only by the wind. Even with a keen eye, the ledges are barely perceptible from seaward; often the tired mind and eye of the ship's lookout isn't sure they are there until it's too late...

Underneath, Poppy had written:

Now, isn't that the truth! Entered in thick fog 8/11/67, at 0600 hours after sailing through the night. Set and strictly followed course in from the sea buoy off the entrance; current must have grabbed us, though, sliding Archaic to the SW, setting us onto one of the outside ledges. Thought we would lose her, but a lobster boy appeared out of the fog and towed us off.

Note: we found, upon leaving several days later that in clear weather it's not so bad; just stay away in fog or darkness.

Cleo shook her head. Some 'lobster boy'! But this was no time for reflection, and she continued to read the detailed entry instructions in the cruising guide, which jogged her memory from so many years before. Poppy's notes in the guide gave her optimism; going in with no fog and even in what would be dwindling daylight should still be fine, she thought.

"Mom, I think I see it. I think I see it," came Sophie's excited shout.

"I'll be right up."

Cleo triple checked the course on the chart, laid from the sea buoy off the entrance into the harbor, then she headed on deck to relieve Sophie at the wheel.

"Mom, it was right there," Sophie said, pointing, "but now it's gone." Cleo looked ahead but all she saw was a flash of lightning shooting through an angry black cloud on the horizon to the southwest.

"Afternoon thunderstorm," Cleo mouthed. "Shit." The last thing they needed was to be assaulted by a squall near those ledges, especially with all this sail up. And if she reduced sail now, they wouldn't have the boat speed to make it in before dark.

She turned to Sophie, who was now leaning forward over the cabin trunk, anxiously scanning the horizon for the island. "Sophie, I think we should head east, out to sea, reduce sail, and ride it out until morning. It's just too…"

"Noooo," Sophie screamed. "You *said*! You said we were going in. I'm sick. I'm shivering. I can't stay up here in the cockpit all night. I'll be even sicker in the cabin. Why did you take me out here at all? Why did you do this to me?"

The storm was coming from the west and heading east, as best Cleo could tell. That's what those July storms off Maine usually did, she thought. And they were headed 330 degrees, north-northwest. Maybe…just maybe, it would track below them. Cleo watched closely, biting her lower lip. It would be a huge relief to make it into Gadus for the night, a night of rest and hopefully one of thoughtful discussion with Sophie about continuing on or returning home. But deep down, Cleo was not relieved; she knew this course would take her deep into the past and then the present could reveal what had become of everything…what had become of him. That scared her. Why didn't she want to know? What did she fear? Maybe it had just been her busy life that got in the way of following up, she thought. But deep down she knew she was fooling herself. She could have at least gotten a message out to him, explaining what happened and what was behind her broken promise. Yet even this year, so many years later, with a course which took them right by Gadus, she had tried to stay away. Was it safer to not know? Safer to let time heal for him, or to at least wear away the past? Yet what about Sophie? Didn't she, of all people, have a right to know?

And now the storm appeared to be tracking more to the southeast; in fact, it appeared to be breaking up. "We're going into Gadus, Sophie! I think we can make it! The storm seems to be falling apart and I just got a glimpse of the island. We're getting close." She looked over at Sophie, who was staring ahead and nodding. "Sweetie, I just need you to take the wheel for two minutes while I check the tide.

I think it will be low water at around seven-thirty, so the ledges will be showing, and we'll still have enough daylight to see them while working our way in."

Back on deck after confirming the low tide time, Cleo took the wheel again. The wind had lightened, the seas had begun to flatten, and steering was now easier. Maybe twenty minutes left to go. She tried to recall a picture of the entrance through the ledges, but instead her mind insisted on replaying the terror of the past, when that undersea ledge, like some monster rising from the deep, had suddenly lifted them from the sea. She remembered the horrific sounds, the thud of rock hitting the lead keel and then the scraping and grinding of the mahogany planks of *Archaic's* bottom as the old sloop slid onto the ledge, rose up and then stopped. Then the silence. The sense that the world had stopped and was about to be over. That they were going to sink. That they were going to drown. And then another sound. An outboard motor somewhere near, but out of sight in the fog. She remembered blowing the foghorn, over and over, while her grandfather Poppy was down in the cabin, seemingly forever, checking the bilge for leaks. And then what she thought for sure was an apparition, a ghostly figure in a boat, slowly coming out of the fog. But not so. It really *was* the shape of a boat with someone standing in it, edging ever closer, but stopping short of coming alongside. The fog-shrouded figure stood silent, staring at them. "Thank you for coming. We're stuck on the ledge," Cleo had shouted. The figure stayed silent. An ocean swell carried his boat a bit closer, almost alongside, and she saw a long-haired, primitive looking, yet handsome teenaged boy in a fishing skiff. A faded, bait-stained picture of a lobster stared out from his worn gray sweatshirt; above the lobster were the words *Stay calm in a pinch.* Hanging from his neck was a cord strung with seal claws, bones, and beads, and tucked under his belt was what looked like a bayonet. He seemed from a different time, odd, anxious, and strangely disengaged. "You'll pull us off?" Cleo had pleaded. The boy reached down to the steering arm of his outboard and for a moment she thought he would turn and just leave them there. But instead, he put the engine in reverse and backed up to *Archaic's* stern. Then he threw a line to her. "Tie it here?" she had asked, gesturing to the stern post on *Archaic*. The boy only nodded, so she cleated the line at the stern and looked up at him and his small outboard, which he'd shut off. "Is your motor strong enough?"

No reply. The boy sat down in his fishing skiff and stared at her. "I don't understand," Cleo had said after several minutes. "I don't see why you're just…"

The boy shook his head before finally speaking. "Tide's coming. Best to wait a bit. Let nature take care of things. No sense ripping your planks out pulling her when she'll float off on her own soon."

And that's what happened. The boy spoke no more. Ten minutes later he'd stood again, started his motor, turned the skiff, and slowly throttled up, taking up tension on the line, and then pulling gently until *Archaic* slid gracefully off the ledge. When *Archaic's* temperamental motor wouldn't start, he'd towed them into the tiny slit of the harbor at Gadus Island.

* * *

Sophie stood now and looked at the island. "Mom, this place looks kind of creepy. Look at that old tower. Like something out of the Middle Ages."

"Maybe you'll find your knight in shining armor here," Cleo said. The irony was not lost on her. She stared at the tower's sharpening outline against the hilly point of land on the island's east side. The last time she had looked at that tower, in 1967, she had been Sophie's age.

Sophie snapped her back. "Where are the ledges, Mom? And where's the harbor?"

"The harbor is very narrow, but once we get around the east side of the island, you'll see it." Cleo looked to the south, just off the island, for the ledges. She could see them now, clearly scraping the surface and erupting in a roiling sea of foam. "There! There are the ledges. Now we're good."

She reached down, turned the ignition key and, fingers crossed—the engine was almost as old as *Archaic*—pushed the starter button. The old Universal Atomic Four gas engine came right to life. "I'll round up into the wind, Sophie, then run forward and drop the jib. We'll keep the mainsail up until we drop anchor, just for insurance if the engine fails."

As they entered the harbor, Cleo was eager to see if things had changed. In 1967 it had been a nearly deserted place, with only an old stone wharf and some stone foundations in the meadow above giving any evidence of former inhabitants. And of course, there was the old mastless sloop. That would be long gone, no doubt. She throttled down to an idle as they reached the inner part of the harbor. She was surprised; not much had changed. The old stone wharf was there. There was a shack behind it; it looked inhabited. There was no mastless sloop. Cleo decided to drop anchor right where the sloop used to be. She had Sophie take the wheel while she went forward and lowered the anchor, then came aft, noted their position off the wharf, and put the boat in reverse, adding some throttle until she was sure the anchor had set. Right then was one of Cleo's favorite moments when cruising, because it was a mixture of good feelings: a sense of safety after finally anchoring in a snug harbor after being at sea; a feeling of fulfillment at having completed the day's run; and a chance to drop her vigilance and relax with a big glass of wine.

But Sophie was in a huff, sitting with her knees up and her head between them, looking down. It was clear she had none of her mother's good feelings. This spoiled things for Cleo; ruined the moment. She knew she should say something calming, pleasant, positive to quell any storm, but instead she tried to justify things. "Look, Sophie, it's just that I thought—about this trip and all—that..."

Sophie pulled her face up from between her knees and glared at her mother. "That what? That putting me on this stupid boat, practically shanghaiing me, then bashing into those stupid waves, wandering about in the stupid fog...what?... that would be good for me? That would be what I needed?"

"Well, what *do* you need?"

No answer.

"Okay. Tomorrow, we'll head back. There. Done."

Cleo had expected at least some small gesture of relief from her daughter that they would be returning, that she was giving in to her wishes. Instead, Sophie put her face down between her knees again, angering Cleo. "Well, until we leave tomorrow, you'll have time to go back to writing in your diary about your horrible mother."

Sophie looked up at Cleo, wide eyed. "Oh my God, are you reading my diary?"

"No, I'm not reading it. I would never do that."

Sophie didn't respond. Food, Cleo thought. She needs food. We both need food to cheer us up. She stood and headed toward the cabin to go below deck to begin supper. Then she turned.

"Sophie, did you really *write* that about me? About me being a horrible mother?"

There was no response.

Supper was to be a salad and a reheated beef stew left over from the previous night. It needed to be quick; they were having supper much later than usual. Cleo opened the heavy oak ice chest lid, grabbed the flashlight that hung from the hook by the sink, and peered into the chest to find the big pink Tupperware cannister. Then it was time to wrestle with the monster: *Archaic's* dreadful old, pressurized alcohol stove. Cleo was amazed these things had never been outlawed. But she was proud of her ability to tame it. She smiled at her memory of the first time Poppy had shown her how to light it; how it caused both amusement and terror.

"Ohkuk, first thing you have to understand is that this stove is like living with a big ugly rabid dog. It's cantankerous and can have a major flare up and bite you if you ever take your eyes off it." Poppy shook his head. "The number of stories about pressurized alcohol fires is almost as large as the number of stories of all other marine disasters combined." He chuckled. "You'll know the folks who have these things on their boats without ever having to go in their cabin. They'll be the ones with no hair on their arms, legs and face. So, let's be careful."

Cleo opened the top of the alcohol tank, grabbed the flashlight, and peered in to see if there was enough fuel. Then she closed the top, pumped up pressure in the fuel tank attached to the stove, then opened the valve on one of the burners for five seconds, letting fuel seep into the holding cup at the base of the burner. Then Cleo took a long wooden match and carefully lit the fuel in the holding cup, letting it heat the burner while burning down. Just when the flame went out, she lit another match, opened the burner valve, and, standing back from the stove as far as possible, touched the match flame to the burner. With a huge whoosh, the burner came to life, but along with it came a foot-high flareup from the excess fuel in the holding cup. Finally, it receded. Cleo shook her head. "Insanity," she mumbled as she placed the stew pot on the burner.

They ate in the cabin after Cleo lit the three kerosene lanterns and put the mosquito screens in place. She knew from experience there was nothing worse than mosquitos trapped inside, ultimately finding your ear at three in the morning. They sat on separate bunks, the varnished cabin table between, and were silent while eating. Cleo had expected that. She wanted food to enter their systems before trying to talk. She also knew that the cabin of a boat was, like the inside of a car, one of those rare places where things get said that otherwise wouldn't, especially by children and teenagers. So, Cleo bided her time while soaking her bread in the stew and planning her approach. She felt the ocean swell gently lifting *Archaic*, the mast and bulkheads creaking slightly. Cleo looked up at Sophie, who was also sopping up her stew. The glow from the lamps on the varnished wood of the cabin gave their small, enclosed space the feeling of a sanctuary. It was a soft, otherworldly feel, and made Sophie's face look angelic. God, Cleo thought, she is everything to me. How she loved her, despite it all! And how she wanted to protect her. But from what? From everything.

"Hey, Soph. Look, I promise I'll get us back home as quickly as I can. Okay? And I want to say thanks for coming, at least this far. It means a lot to me. I'm sorry for thinking this would be…well, I can see it must seem weird, a teenaged girl going to sea on an old wooden boat with her …"

Sophie put down the remains of her bread, looked up. "…her divorced mother."

"We've been over this, Sophie. It's better this way."

"So, it's better to break up a family into three pieces? How's that working out for all of us?"

"Yes, I think it is, in the long run. It wasn't me who…"

"Forget it." Sophie got up, put her plate and glass in the sink, turned and went forward to her cabin. Cleo stood, rinsed the dishes, and poured another glass of wine. The mosquitoes would be gone now, this long after dusk, so she removed the main hatch screen, and climbed the steps to the cockpit. She sat and faced the stone wharf; nearby, in the shack she'd seen while coming in, a light burned dimly in the one window. Maybe the island now had a caretaker, and he—or she—was in there. Doing what?

Then a striking memory: she and Poppy motor sailing away from this same island, all those years ago, the two of them staring at a lone figure on the hill by the tower.

* * *

Now, so many years later, she stared at the dimly lit window in the shoreside shack, and wondered aloud. "Maybe. Just maybe. No, couldn't be." Then she rose, carefully making her way forward to check the anchor before heading into the cabin to wash up and get ready for bed. From her stance in the bow, she could look down through the forward hatch into Sophie's cabin; the lantern was still aglow, though Sophie appeared to be sound asleep in the V-shaped double bunk. She was sleeping on her side, zipped up in her sleeping bag, her favorite baby blue pillow bunched up under her head.

How many nights had Cleo slept in that same bunk, either lying on her back looking up at the old deck beams, or lying on her side facing the strong oak ribs of the hull. She always felt so secure up there in the bow under those strong oak beams, knowing that Poppy was right back in the main cabin. Until that trip to Gadus in 1967, when they'd almost been lost on the ledge, she'd always thought he was infallible, that he could handle anything at sea, fight the biggest storms, fix *Archaic*'s worst structural or mechanical problems, navigate through the densest fog. Things were so different now.

Cleo sat down on the cabin top, leaned back against the old spruce mast, and looked up at the stars. When she was about ten, Poppy had shown her how to find the summer constellations, including Ursa Major, Ursa Minor, the North Star, Cassiopeia, and the Summer Triangle, a trio of bright stars that included Deneb.

"Maybe your nickname should be Deneb instead of Ohkuk," he'd said, his voice chock full of pride for his little granddaughter.

She'd given him a funny look. Cocked her head. "Huh?"

"Well, makes sense, my dear. Deneb is one of the most luminous stars — about 200,000 times brighter than the sun. Like you!"

It made her think of their special 'archeology Saturdays,' when they went back in time together, learning about the ways of ancient peoples. Cleo closed her eyes and took herself back to one particular Saturday in 1960.

III

An 'Archeology Saturday' – 1960
Dr. Bion Taylor's Home,
Marblehead, Massachusetts

The nine year old leans into the heavy oak front door, pushes it open and charges through the front hall into the den. Despite a purple backpack so full of books it threatens to pull her over, she falls forward into the big chair and hugs her grandfather, nearly knocking a semi-translucent light grey stone from his hand. "Ah, Ohkuk, you have returned to my world! Your dad here? Your dad coming in?"

"No, Poppy, he said he's in a hurry. So, what are you looking at? And where are we going for our adventure today? And is there any *pizza*?"

"Well, my dear Ohkuk, I'll answer those in order: I'm studying one of the Ramah chert projectile points from my collection." He holds it up to the light for her.

"You can almost see right through the stone, Poppy. Cool."

"The shamans of the Red Paint People were fond of translucent materials like this, as they believed they evoked their special ability to see into and beyond objects." He looks up at the ceiling, a thought forming. "You know, beyond that, I was thinking: the manual archaeological projectile point morphological classification is an extensive and complex process that has real meaning."

Now on the floor with her backpack, wrestling with one of its zippers, the girl furrows her brow. "Poppy, is it an extensive and complex process to fix this darned stuck zipper? I have something in here to give you…Wait, I got it. Fixed the zipper, Poppy!" She unzips and pulls out a white paper bag and hands it to her grandfather. "It's from my dad. A birthday present." Poppy pulls a t-shirt out of the bag, holds it up, and stares at it:

archaeologist

noun [ahr-kee-ol-uh-jist]

1. A crackpot digging up cracked pots
2. Will date any old thing
3. Has a career that always ends up in ruins

"How thoughtful."

"It's silly and kind of mean, I think. But mine's the best, Poppy. Not done yet though. I'm making something special for you, but it's not finished."

"Well, why don't we take Saturday's journey back in time from out on the sunporch today, shall we Ohkuk? Such a nice day. And then we can warm up some pizza I have left over from last night… or maybe it was from last week, or was it…well…anyway, I'm sure it's fine."

Out on the porch, she sits in her favorite wicker chair, her elbows on the arm rests, her fists under her chin, and leans forward intently. "Tell me the story of the real Ohkuk and the island again. Pleaseeee Poppy Bion."

"Well, it was about 4000 years ago, Cleo."

Cleo smiles. "That's sure a lot older than even you, Poppy!"

"Yes, my dear, considerably."

"Anyway, Ohkuk was one of the Red Paint People on what is now the coast of Maine. She was a red-headed girl of fourteen, and that day she moved slowly up the rise of land, eyes down, searching for edible wild plants. She was clothed in animal skins sewn together with an intricately crafted bone needle, and with thread fashioned from plant materials. And the rows of seal claws, small bone pendants, and beads were more than decoration of her hide clothing; Ohkuk believed they had magical power, as did she. In fact, her name *meant* 'magic power'. And because of her red hair, she was treated like

31

royalty, because her hair looked like fire and fire was a great power to these people. In fact, women with red hair often became the wives of the chieftains."

Cleo fluffs up her wavy reddish hair. "So, *I* could marry a chief?"

"Perhaps."

"Wait! Why wouldn't I *be* the chief? I'm the one with the red hair!"

"Well, I suppose…"

"How does the magic work, anyway?"

"Well, she has to believe. Just to believe for it to work." Poppy thinks deeply, slipping back into his former world of academia. "It was believed by a tribe of Native Americans that this was an extraordinary invisible power and pervaded in varying degrees all animate and inanimate natural objects as a transmissible spiritual energy capable of being exerted according to the will of its possessor, a successful hunter's 'orenda' which overcomes that of his quarry."

Cleo shakes her head, gives her 'silly smile'. "There you go again, Poppy. I know you say I'm a smart cookie, but I'm still a little cookie; you're talking again like you're teaching in your college school."

"Sorry."

"Is this invisible power like a magic show? Did they have those four thousand years ago?"

"Well, they had magic. There's always been magic. Life is magic. Anyway, Ohkuk had wandered away from her band, and was absently searching for plants, but mostly her eyes looked seaward. Her mind was lost in thought; she worried about a strong young man in her band of hunter gatherers, a man who had been gone too long in the big dugout that chased the great swordfish. She gently fingered her beads, tried to calm herself by believing that the shaman, the captain of the big dugout, would use his magic to protect them."

"I thought Ohkuk had the magic? She should use it to bring back this boy. Why does she need this shaman guy? Is he her boyfriend maybe? Girls had boyfriends back then, right, Poppy?"

"Oh, yes. Girls had boyfriends. But let me continue, Cleo. You see, we don't know much about The Red Paint People, but we do know some things. It's possible there was an Ohkuk or someone like her doing what Ohkuk does in my story because of what we know."

"How do we know just some things?"

"Well, because…"

"I know why! Because of archeology. Like you. Because of archeologists. They dig."

"Yes, we know from digs, and from what we find in shell middens and graves."

"Shell middens? Is that what shells wear on their hands in cold weather?"

"Very cute, Ohkuk. Shell middens are cultural spaces found on the mainland and island

coasts. They were created by Maine's Indigenous People during thousands of years of coastal occupation. To archeologists they are a rich source of information on prehistoric lifestyles."

"What about the graves? Have you ever done a grave dig, Poppy? What would be the best thing to find if we did one?"

"Well, yes, I have done many digs, Cleo, and I suppose…" Bion closed his eyes; his mind took him away, away 12,000 years.

"Although the archaeological record in Maine is far from complete, it suggests a scattering of small, mobile hunting bands. The Paleo-indian's signature tool was a large, fluted projectile point mounted on a spear and launched with a spear-thrower, or atlatl. Now that would be a find!"

"An atlatl? Silly word. But cool! An ancient spear thrower! Can we go find that one? Please! Let's get on the boat and sail to Maine to do a dig next summer. To find one of those atlatls. And Red Paint People stuff."

"Well, I'd like that. I'd like doing that with you, Cleo. But your father, I'm afraid, wouldn't permit it. At least not until you're older. But I'm sure the Red Paint People will wait until…"

"Why *are* they called Red Paint People anyway?"

"That's what I was going to tell you. It's because when they died and were buried, this material called red ocher, a kind of red powder, was found in their graves. We're not sure why they did that."

"Like paprika? Why would they do that? It seems silly."

"We're not sure. They were amongst the strangest and most ignored ancient peoples that archeologists have studied. Many who have studied them have made claims about their age and technology that others felt were outlandish."

"What's 'outlandish'?"

"Eccentric."

She folded her hands together under her chin, and leaned toward her grandfather. "My dad says you're that."

"Oh. Well…what do you think?"

She stood up abruptly, putting her hands on her hips. "Poppy, I don't know. I just learned that word five seconds ago, for Pete's sake."

"Well then, smart cookie, you should practice using it. It's the best way to learn new words. What? What are you smiling about?"

"That's just 'outlandish', Poppy."

"What is?"

"That a little kid like me would be expected to use such a big word." She smirks and tilts her head.

Bion shakes his head and smiles.

"Gotcha!" she says, raising a fist in the air. "And now: pizza!"

Bion shakes his head again, in an exaggerated manner. "Instead, how about we heat up some stale crackers, pour soy sauce on them, and sprinkle some garlic flakes on the top?"

"Now, *that's* 'outlandish,' Poppy."

"Eccentric."

"Exactly."

IV

July 8, 1985
Gadus Island Harbor

leo awoke the next morning to find their world embraced by a blurry soft white cocoon of fog. Without sitting up, she could look aft through the cabin hatch and see its thickness. She knew Sophie would be frustrated and angry about their being trapped for one or more days by this fog. She thought of what Poppy had said to her years ago when she'd become frustrated by the fog's tenacity. He'd simply smiled and said, "Everything is still right there, like always. It just takes patience and vigilance to bring you through. Remember, Cleo, beyond the fog lies clarity."

She knew there was no hurry now; they wouldn't be leaving anytime soon. But there *was* a hurry to try to piece together and make some sense of last night's dream. (Somewhere she'd read that one only had about ten minutes after awakening before 90% of a dream is gone.) She pulled the grey wool blanket over her head, closed her eyes, and remembered: Wearing only animal skins for clothing, she was standing in the stern of a large dugout canoe. She was talking to a giant swordfish. About what, she couldn't remember, but it seemed urgent. The swordfish had a gold ring on the tip of its long sword, and its eyes were flashing neon arrows pointing seaward. As it rolled in the sea it lifted one of its lower fins in a gesture for her to follow. Then it dove. Disappeared. Then reappeared, airborne, free of the sea. Before landing, the head had turned. But it was a different head this time. A human one. With a face of someone she once knew, but an older face now.

She sat up abruptly. The fog outside the companionway hatch seemed to be getting even thicker; she could barely see the steering wheel now in the aft end of the cockpit. Oddly—or maybe not—Cleo wondered what the ancient people, what the Red Paint People, had believed about fog. Was it an invader? Why did it come to shut out their world? Why did it always go away? Why did it never hurt them? And what did their shamans say about it?

She thought back to her first real fog experience, as a teenager at sea with Poppy. It had been a persistent, thick fog on their way to Maine from Massachusetts aboard *Archaic*. They'd left The Isles of Shoals off Portsmouth and the fog stuck to them all day, showing no signs of letting up. They were moving slowly and carefully under power, the old Atomic Four gas engine leaving a trail of white exhaust which mixed with the fog before disappearing in their wake. With nothing to see or hear except the throbbing of the engine, she'd gotten bored after a couple hours, so she'd asked Poppy to tell her another story of ancient peoples.

"Well, this won't be truly ancient my dear. But it's local to where we are, and certainly timely and appropriate given this eerie fog."

Poppy began telling her about the early days of fishing on the bleak islands of 'the Shoals'. "In 1873, there was a hardy pioneering Norwegian fisherman named John Hontvet and his wife Maren who lived alone on Smuttynose Island, one of the Isles of Shoals. Later they were joined by Karen, Maren's sister, who had also emigrated from Norway. Last to join the growing family in the small house were Maren's brother Ivan and his beautiful new bride Anethe. It was an isolated, lonely, and hard way to eke out a living, fishing off the remote small island. But it was better than the starvation that had faced them in Norway. Slowly things seemed to get better; John was saving money and Maren was less lonely with the two women with her now, especially while John and Ivan were at sea. One day John and Ivan had to sail into Portsmouth for bait, which was arriving by train from Boston. The train was late, forcing them to spend the night tied to the wharf in Portsmouth, leaving the three women alone on Smuttynose for the night. John had faith that the women would be fine without the men for just one night. But Louis Wagner—an out-of-worker drifter and former fisherman of the Isles of Shoals who had once stayed on with the Hontvets for a short period after Ivan and Anethe had arrived—learned of the situation. He stole a dory and rowed the ten miles to Smuttynose, most likely with robbery and perhaps rape on his mind. Things went horribly wrong; two of the three women, Anethe and Karen, were brutally murdered by ax in the pre-dawn hours. Maren escaped and ran barefooted in her nightshirt to the other end of the island, hiding in a cave while clinging to her small dog. Louis Wagner searched for Maren, the only living witness, but figured she would die of exposure and, fearing the light of day, he rowed back to Portsmouth."

Cleo remembered being aghast. "Poppy, that can't be the end of the story. Don't leave me hanging!"

Poppy gave a half smile. "It was Louis Wagner who was left hanging, my dear. By the neck, after they caught him."

"Wow, a good creepy story."

"Yes, and a *true* creepy story. It's all documented."

"Creepy like this fog," Cleo had said. She shook her head, then looked around at the nothingness. "What good is fog, anyway?"

Poppy had thought for a while. "Well, it's certainly good for literature," he'd said. "Fog is good for plot. It's transcendent. It's sensuous, plays tricks with the eye and perception. With fog, writers can make their characters lose control of their world. Think about Dickens: *Bleak House, A Christmas Carol, Great Expectations.* Think of Robert Louis Stevenson's *Dr Jekyll and Mr Hyde.* And, oh my, of course Arthur Conan Doyle's *Hound of the Baskervilles.* Poppy had wiped some moisture from his thick white eyebrows before continuing.

"And I believe it was Melville, visiting London, who was the first to record the words "pea soup" in relation to the fog. Why, fog is itself almost another character in literature."

Cleo smiled at the memory as she flipped off her blanket, swung her legs down from the bunk, and thought about how she was probably the only person on earth who had written a dissertation on the topic of fog and literature. It was Poppy who had first planted that seed, ultimately leading to her career, tenuous as it now was, as an associate professor of literature.

But better to think about coffee, about lighting the dreaded stove, and about keeping it going after coffee to dry out the cabin using Poppy's ingenious and safe 'brick method'. She got up and went aft, her bare feet feeling the dampness of the floorboards, and opened the small cabinet under the stove. She was pleased to find the old brick still there. "It's simple," Poppy had said. "Before you go ashore on a foggy morning, you put this brick on the burner and get it as hot as possible, then you turn off the stove, close up all the hatches, and row ashore. When you return, you'll find the cabin dry and cozy, because that little brick will have absorbed almost all of the moisture while you were ashore. And no danger from fire whatsoever!"

Going ashore: that had bounced around in Cleo's mind since she'd first decided to reverse their course the prior afternoon. It would have to wait, though. She knew Sophie wouldn't stir for a while. And Cleo would need to be there when she awakened. She would need to be there to calm what would be Sophie's angry reaction to the fog and its obvious message that they weren't going anywhere anytime soon.

Well, Cleo would start by making a good breakfast. Then she'd build from there.

Sophie finally arose and came aft. She sat on the seat across from the galley, rubbed her eyes, then pulled back and wrestled with her long black hair before wrapping a turquoise scrunchie around it. "Mom, what time are we leaving?" she asked, without looking up.

"Did you look out the hatch?"

"What?"

"Thick fog. We're stuck for a bit, Sophie. But…"

Sophie picked up Poppy's old logbook and slammed it back down on the table. "Shit!"

Cleo caught her breath, gave Sophie her kindest smile and, in the nicest tone she could muster, said "Sweetie, I don't make the weather. But you know what? My grandfather Poppy would see this positively, as an opportunity; he'd say: 'Fog gives us a chance to look inward, and then, when it lifts, there's clarity'."

Sophie glared at Cleo. "Poppy, Poppy, Poppy. Everything's Poppy. Why don't you ever rattle on about *my* father, or about your own father…who is *my* grandfather." Cleo put down the banana she was peeling, and sat on the bunk behind Sophie's seat at the navigation table. She reached out tentatively, then gently smoothed her daughter's hair that hung below the scrunchie.

"It's because it was Poppy who was kind. It was my grandfather who truly cared, who taught me about what was important in life. About what was good. He taught me to be curious. Poppy was the one who was always there for me, Soph. And that's what I'm trying to do for you. To be there for you." She gently rubbed the top of Sophie's head. "To love you." She hoped Sophie's downcast eyes would meet hers. When they didn't, Cleo turned and looked through the hatch, through her tears, and into the fog. Then she turned back to Sophie. "My father wasn't there for me. Or there for you, as a grandfather.

42

And as for your dad, well, things happened that made it better to be apart, Sophie. I'm sorry. But I can't change that. I can only try to make sure what happens now and what happens next is good for you. And for me."

Sophie's eyes narrowed. She cocked her head. "So why did you and Dad stay together so long?"

Cleo took a breath. "Because of you, Sophie. Two parents seemed best. But also, we were so young. I was pregnant, still eighteen. We needed each other. Or so we thought. So, we got married. You were born at the end of our freshman year. It was a tough time. A crazy time. There was a war. Vietnam. I'd been really involved in protests against it, and writing columns critical of the war for the school paper. Leading marches. Taking English classes. And then, well, with you coming and all, I had to drop out."

Sophie shook her head and smirked. "Sorry, Mom."

"Sophie, no, no. Listen, I did what I thought was best. I put you first; I put things on hold for you. Which was fine. Which was best for then. But, you know, I had also really loved being a literature major and writer. I wanted to teach at a college someday. It wasn't until you were in grade school that I could swing it to go back and get my degrees. Even then, your dad—"

"He what?"

"He didn't want me to go back. It's as if he didn't want me to get ahead. Or leave the apartment, for that matter. Just like he didn't want me to protest the war the year we met. We were different that way. And then, later on, his job kept moving us around."

Sophie smirked again. "Yeah, that was fun, huh?"

Cleo gave her daughter a commiserating smile, tried to lighten things. "You mean glorious winters in Albany?"

Sophie shook her head and half smiled in memory. "Yeah, and weirdos in Wichita Falls."

"Anyway, sweetie, I did the best I could. I tried to make it as harmonious as possible. But I so missed the ocean and Poppy. And *Archaic*. It was great to land back in Marblehead finally. And I know you love it there, too."

Sophie was silent. The only sounds were the seemingly countless ticks of the old brass ship's clock, which had hung for years next to its companion barometer on the bulkhead. 'Some hearts understand each other, even in silence,' Cleo thought—she prayed it would be so. Finally, Sophie picked up the logbook in front of her, turned it over carefully, smoothed out the bent pages, then tried to dry them with her hand as they became blotted with tears.

The time felt right. Cleo took a chance. "There's something else. Something happened here, Sophie—I mean right here, on this island—a long time ago. It was all so strange. Like in a dream. But not." Sophie turned on her seat and faced her mother, silent and staring. Cleo stared into her daughter's eyes; they were such striking, piercing eyes, eyes that always took her aback when she looked too far into them. "I was your age," Cleo continued. "And I've never shared it with anyone. Even Poppy. But it's very very important to finally share it with you; you more that anyone." Cleo's voice was tight. It cracked while she spoke. Her daughter looked scared. She wiped her blue cotton pajama sleeve across her wet eyes. "Mom? Oh my God. What? What?"

Cleo paused. Shook her head. "I've kept it buried inside. From fear. From guilt." She hesitated again. "Maybe from love. But I want to tell you. I need to tell you. Maybe together, we can…we can both understand."

Sophie was wide-eyed. "Me? Mom, what!?...I don't..."

They heard a sudden swishing sound. Then it came again. Cleo shot up. "Someone's out there," she said, climbing the cabin steps to look out into the fog. Sophie got up, moved to the port side of the cabin, pressed her nose against the glass of one of the portholes, and peered out. The swishing continued. But she could see nothing. "A fish. Maybe a big fish," Sophie said. "Or a whale. God, maybe it's a whale."

"In here? In this tiny harbor?"

Sophie pulled her head away, and wiped her breath off the fogged up porthole glass. There was a thump on the port side of the hull. Both she and her mother froze. "What was *that*?" Sophie asked. She looked back through the porthole, her eyes inches from the glass, as part of a hand—four white, wrinkly fingers—emerged, hooking itself over the rail cap on *Archaic's* deck. Sophie let out a shriek that seemed to shatter their foggy world, reverberating throughout *Archaic* and the harbor of Gadus Island. She shot into the forward cabin, slammed and locked the door, wrapped her arms around herself, and hyperventilated.

A few moments later a voice arose from the water along *Archaic's* port side. "Hello. Ah, hello on board *Archaic*. Ah, sorry if I startled."

A young man's head, barely more than an outline in the fog, appeared just above *Archaic's* rail. Cleo stood frozen at the top of the main hatch steps, staring at the man's face as if he were an apparition. "You terrified us both."

"Again, sorry. It's hard to do anything *but* sneak up in a fog like this."

"Well, there's always the idea of making a bit of noise in advance. Or how about 'hello' or 'excuse me' when you're some ways off. We thought you were either a whale or a ghost."

The young man smiled sheepishly, while still sitting in the skiff and hanging to the rail. The two looked across at each other, neither saying anything for a few moments. Then he stood up carefully in the rowing skiff. "Actually, there was, or are, ghosts. Here, actually, in fact, on the island, they say," he said, his voice assuming a tone of local knowledge and authority. His diction and redundancy reminded Cleo of some of her freshman composition students, which always bugged her. Plus, she was still perturbed by the boy's sudden shocking arrival.

"Actually? Is that *actually* so. An *actual* fact? Well, at least it's not you. Being the ghost, I mean," Cleo said, sliding her hand across her forehead in a phew! gesture. Cleo moved up to the cockpit, grabbed a cushion, turned its fog-wet side over, and sat down near the rail by the young man. "You must be from the shack ashore? Otherwise…I mean, I think we're the only boat in here." Closer to him now, she could see a depth in his eyes, a gentleness, a soulfulness. He was tall and seemed agile, easily balancing in the skiff as a slight swell rolled into the harbor. He wore grey gym shorts and a maroon hooded sweatshirt emblazoned with *1985 World Environment Day* across the front.

"I'm the caretaker here on Gadus for the summer. It's part of my environmental internship. I'm focusing on sustainable living, marine organisms and their environment. Anyway, I just wanted to come out and check on you, see if all was okay."

"I bet. Especially after you heard that bloodcurdling scream!"

"Well, no. Actually, that occurred after I…"

"I know. I know. We're fine," Cleo said. "But thank you." He seemed like a good kid; Cleo thought she should back down. She'd been playing with him, the way she had sometimes messed with her students in class when they tried to take on an air of sophistication in their speech or when they overwrote, using redundant words and phrases such as: absolutely essential, actual fact, at this point in time, eliminate entirely, or end result.

"Well, I'm sorry I made you scream."

"Oh, that was my daughter. She's still hiding in the forward cabin."

"Then please tell her I'm sorry." He looked into the nothingness around him, shaking his head like a wise old mariner. "I think we're going to be socked in for a while. Glad you made it in last night before it dropped on us. You're welcome to come ashore if you'd like. I can show you around. There's quite a history. And I'm pretty proud of my garden; I could show you that. And I could show you some of the artifacts I've collected for the little museum shed the Conservation Land Trust has set up, and also..."

Sophie's head of black hair slowly rose, then her face appeared in the main hatch, catching his attention.

"Oh, hello. Hey, sorry I scared you."

Sophie studied the young man while pushing some stray hairs back over her ears. "It's okay. I guess. It's just that I was looking through the porthole and suddenly these creepy white waterlogged fingers slithered up on the rail, like some sea monster or from some Stephen King flick."

He looked at his hands. "Oh. Yeah. That *would* be kind of creepy. You see, I'm wet a lot. I mean, bailing the skiff. And pulling up echinoderms..."

"Echino what?"

"Oh, well, you see, echinoderms are members of the phylum echinodermata of marine animals. The adults are recognizable by their radial symmetry, and include starfish, sea urchins, sand dollars, and sea cucumbers, as well as the sea lilies." He looked back at his fingers. "I can show you if you'd like. In fact, here in the skiff…" He bent down, then dropped out of sight.

Sophie looked at her mother. Rolled her eyes.

When he reappeared, he was holding what looked like a hairy, dull brown cucumber with a bunch of finger-like tentacles around its mouth. "This is a sea cucumber. *Cucumaria frondose.*"

Sophie recoiled. "Maybe you shouldn't touch it."

"Oh, actually, it's fine to touch. In fact, you can eat it. Some people even eat them raw."

Sophie turned her chin down, looked away, and closed her eyes.

"Very interesting," Cleo said. "Well, thank you for stopping by. We have some chores to finish now, so…"

"Oh, sure. And my name's Cary. Cary Thompson." He leaned over the rail, put the sea cucumber down on the deck, and reached out to shake hands."

Cleo and Sophie leaned back slightly from Cary, lifting their right hands in a half wave rather than risking a handshake. "I'm Cleo and this is Sophie. So nice to meet you. And I'm sure we'll see you later."

As Cary rowed away, Sophie looked wide-eyed at her mother before putting a hand to her mouth, trying to stifle her laughter. "Oh my God, Mom. We come all this way, get trapped in the fog by a remote island, and all alone, and this really cute guy my age suddenly appears from nowhere, and…and… AND HE'S A TOTAL NERD." They both turned toward Cary, who was slowly disappearing, consumed by the fog.

Cleo looked at her daughter. "Holy sea cucumber, Soph. Don't let that one get away!"

They both began laughing uncontrollably. Something they badly needed to do together, and hadn't done in a very long time.

* * *

After a breakfast of corned beef hash and eggs, Sophie climbed a couple steps on the ladder and poked her head out of the hatch to see if the fog had started to lift. If anything, it had gotten worse. Cleo was finishing scrubbing the frying pan. "Can you dry, please, Sophie?" Sophie backed down the ladder, grabbed a plate and the dish towel, and stood by the counter near her mother. "So, what *did* happen to you out here when you were my age?"

Cleo continued to scrub, not responding. When she finished scrubbing, she pumped the galley freshwater lever and gave the pan a quick rinse. "It's best if I show you. Then tell you. All of it. So…so you can see. Maybe understand why. So, anyway, we need to go ashore."

Sophie put down the dry plate next to the sink. Cocked her head. "Don't tell me there was a boy out here for you too, Mom? Or is this about those ghosts that Cucumber Boy was talking about?"

Cleo looked distant now. Haunted. She turned slowly, looked out the hatch into the fog before turning back, very serious, and staring at her daughter. "It's not funny. None of this. Not at all."

"Okay. Okay." Sophie leaned back, away from her mother, raising both hands as if in surrender. Or in fear.

* * *

"Mom, how are you going to show me the shore when we can't even *find* the shore?" Sophie asked, as they shoved off from *Archaic* in the little wooden skiff.

"Pick a direction, cup your hands around your mouth like a megaphone, shout 'boo' a couple times, and then listen carefully," Cleo said, as she slid the oars into the skiff's oarlocks.

Sophie shook her head. "Mom, you're totally losing it."

"No, really. Try it."

Sophie cupped her hands, turned her head to face the left side of the skiff, and shouted 'boo' two times. The sound dissipated into the fog. "I feel like an idiot."

"Now turn 90 degrees and try it again."

Reluctantly, Sophie repeated the process. "Whoa! That bounced back at me."

"That's the land. The other direction on your first try was the harbor opening. No bounce back. You're using your voice like a radar."

"Wait…how did you know…no, never mind." She smirked. "I get it. Poppy showed you."

Cleo smiled at her daughter and started rowing. "So here we go. We'll either come up on one side of the harbor or the other, but at least we won't be out in the three thousand mile-wide Atlantic Ocean." Cleo concentrated. "The trick is to try to row straight; best way to do that in the fog is to watch our wake astern to see if it's straight as I row. Not far to go though."

Sophie was nervous, and looked back toward *Archaic*, but the big sloop had already been swallowed by the fog. "God, Mom. If we miss shore and row out into the ocean in this little boat, we'll drown."

"We won't. Just sit still and concentrate on all those good senses of yours: sight, sound, and smell. You'll be able to smell the land, the seaweed on the rocks, hear the swell rolling onto the shore, and soon…" Cleo paused. She had never seen Sophie so alert, her eyes wide, her nose up, her head cocked and lifted like an animal trying to pull in a scent or sound.

And then: "There's something! I see something. There's a blurry shape. Keep going, Mom. Keep going."

Cleo smiled and finished her statement: "…and soon you'll see land." Like in the slow twisting of the spyglass lens, the blurry shape became more defined, then transformed into a shack perched on the rocky shore. Cleo knew that the wharf and ladder were down harbor from the shack, so when she was almost touching the shore in the skiff, she turned and followed the coast until they spied the wharf. It was low tide, and about twelve feet of the slimy rungs of the ladder were exposed, along with the rest of the underworld of the dilapidated stone wharf. Bright green, almost fluorescent seaweed covered the pink granite ledge at the base of the wharf's barnacle-encrusted pilings. An abandoned lobster boat, half its bottom planks gone, leaned against the wharf, its keel in the mud, waiting for a tide which would never lift it. Sophie grabbed the bottom rung as Cleo maneuvered the skiff to the ladder. Then she let go, looking aghast at her hand. "Yuk. Gross."

Cleo grabbed the side of the ladder, steadying the small boat. "It's the only way up, Soph. You need to go up slowly. It's real slippery. Be careful." As Sophie ascended, Cleo heard the voice of a young man. It wasn't Cary. It wasn't real. It was in her head, a boy's voice from years ago cautioning her about going down the wharf ladder at low tide. "It hurts to slip and fall. I slipped once; my back crashed down onto the rough edge of one of my boat's plywood seats." He'd laughed then, she remembered. A rare, unusual laugh. 'Haaaa haaaa'—a laugh like a raven. "Next thing I knew I was sliding into the dirty bilge water in the bottom of my skiff, landing there like some large freshly caught codfish. I was okay that time. Can't make mistakes like that way out here. At least not more than one."

"Why not more than one," Cleo remembered asking.

"Well, there's this saying: 'Out in the wild you're allowed one mistake. Just one. Because the second one—that's the one that kills you.'"

* * *

"What about Cucumber Boy?" Sophie asked, after Cleo joined her at the top of the wharf. "Should we see him first? Maybe get him to show us around the island?"

Cleo was abrupt. She didn't want anyone with them. "I know this island. We don't need a tour guide. Even in the fog." She pointed into the blurry landscape ahead. Sophie looked where she pointed and shrugged. "Creepy."

"It's this way to the trail leading north," Cleo said. She moved forward and Sophie followed, occasionally looking back to the caretaker shack that was slowly disappearing.

Memories flooded in as Cleo walked toward the north trail. Moving among the island's grasses and sedges, she saw again the flora and fauna she'd marveled at years ago: the ferns, pasture roses, sheep laurel, goldenrod, asters, mosses, and lichens. And around them she heard the different species of birds she'd learned about.

Sophie interrupted Cleo's thoughts. "Mom, I see something ahead. What the…!? That's the *museum*?"

Cleo nodded.

"Mom, it's a shack. And how can you have a museum in a place where there are no people?"

"Just come in and let's see."

The museum, about twelve feet wide and eight feet deep, was sided with old barnboard and driftwood. It had one small six-pane window and a barnboard door with long rusty black hinges and a wooden latch. The roof consisted of several warped panels of tin, extended over a simple deck, to make a small porch.

The door squeaked on its hinges as Cleo stepped through. The scent of salt air and low tide, caught amidst the drifting fog, followed her in. A gull flew over the shack, its screaming call making Sophie hesitate, as if heeding a warning, before she poked her head inside. Crudely displayed on roughly-made shelves were artifacts ranging from the not-so-distant past—early fishing floats, tools and nets, metal farming implements—to things from way back into the Late Archaic period beginning 5,000 years ago. Here were ancient wood-shaping tools, barbed harpoons, bayonets, stone pendants, spear points, and animal hide scrapers. Cleo moved through each piece carefully, not noticing that Sophie had quickly tired of the display and now stared out the small window. "Your great grandfather taught me to be curious, Sophie; he taught me that being curious was one of the most important attributes a person could have. That's why I wanted to come here to this island when I was your age. That's why I explored this island for its past. Like these artifacts." Cleo picked up a long, harpoon-like fish bill. "Sophie? Look. This is an actual swordfish rostrum. It's bone. Poppy told me they were used as foreshafts mounted at the ends of wooden harpoon shafts and armed with bone harpoon tips. He thought they were used for swordfish hunting by the Red Paint People. Back then, several thousands of years ago, he said the surface water was warm enough to allow swordfish to swim inshore around the Gulf of Maine. Now they're way out there; you have to go far offshore to catch one."

Sophie glanced at the artifacts in the small room. Smirked. Turned to face Cleo. "So, what's the next stop on the tour, Mom? Or is this the secret you wanted to show me? Is this what I need to understand?"

"I just thought…Anyway, there's more. I just wanted you to see…"

"See what?" Sophie shrugged. "See what? Mom, what's *with* you? I'm not interested in this stuff. Can't people be interested in what they want?"

Cleo turned away from her daughter, stared out the small window, a blank, almost trance-like look on her face. "On the other side of the island," she continued finally. "It's on the other side of the island. This is the way I came when I first… Look, Sophie, I just need you to understand how it came to…"

Sophie was exasperated. And a bit scared. "Came to WHAT? What *happened* here? Mom, you're freaking me out! Why can't you just *tell* me?"

"I can. And I will." Cleo looked deep into her daughter. "You know I love you more than anything, Sophie."

Sophie threw up her hands. "This is whacked. I'm going back to the wharf. I'll wait there. You go do whatever on the other side of the island." And with that she turned on her heels, stepped out of the museum shack and slowly began to feel her way through the fog along the path back to the wharf. Just before the fog swallowed her, she turned and looked back. "And watch out for those ghosts, Mom. Or whatever it is you're looking for."

* * *

The more steps Sophie took as she walked away from her mother and the museum shack, the more guilty she felt. Curious, too. But also scared. What in the world was her mother trying to tell her? As Sophie walked on, she soon dropped that thought for another: Cucumber Boy. He would most likely be in his cabin by the wharf. Avoid him? Well, he *was* pretty cute, if you could get past his nerdiness. She'd been looking down, walking slowly and carefully through the long grass. Now she looked up and ahead. She couldn't see very far in the fog; that scared her. But if she just followed the path, well… Or was this the right path? It didn't look that familiar. Were there others? Had she wandered onto one? Maybe she should call out for Cucumber Boy? She flashed on his white slithering fingers outside the porthole. No. Maybe she should backtrack? If this was the wrong path it had to lead back to the other path she'd been on. A piercing squawk interrupted her thoughts. Then another. Then a whoosh close by her head. Sophie fell to the ground. Her heart pounded. She realized what it was. In the early part of their trip, her mother had told her that she should stay away from gull nesting areas, that the chicks were born in early summer, stayed in the nest for five or six weeks, and the mothers were very protective at that time, even dive bombing humans to keep them away. And she'd told her about 'cani-gulls'. "When the gulls first hatch, the chicks start to wander around," she'd said. "And the mother's next door neighbors will actually try to eat the other chicks, swallowing them in one gulp. The piercing noise you can sometimes hear will often be a brave parent standing in the face of danger to protect its kids from being eaten alive." Another gull dove at Sophie. This time, she didn't fall; she put her hands over her head and ran. It wasn't long until the blurred outline of the caretaker shack appeared. She *had* been on the right trail. She slowed to a walk, catching her breath, smoothing her hair and wiping the sweat from her forehead with her shirtsleeve while looking intently at the cabin as it became more defined in the fog. Suddenly she wanted company. Even Cucumber Boy.

Tentatively, she moved closer to the caretaker shack, stepping around an outdoor fire pit, over some odd looking tubes and instruments, and around to the shack's door. He didn't seem to be around, so she wandered over to the wharf to see if his skiff was still there. By the wharf's edge she peered down through the fog. His boat was there, empty and tied next to *Archaic's* skiff, so she returned to the shack, deciding to sit in the paint chipped Adirondack chair by the door and wait. Her thoughts drifted to her friends in her hometown of Marblehead, and their plan to attend the upcoming Crosby, Stills and Nash concert on Boston Common—the one she was now sure she would miss. Stupid fog, this stupid trip, she thought angrily. Just then a Monarch butterfly alighted on her arm. Sophie sat still, transfixed by its colors, the deep orange wings, the delicate black borders and the white spots along the edges. Its tiny spherical head was still, seemingly relaxed or resting. The butterfly looked so comfortable on her arm.

"I always thought they should call them flutterbys rather than butterflies."

Sophie looked up, startled. He was shirtless, holding a garden hoe. "Did it again didn't I? I scared you. So sorry. Again."

She looked down at the butterfly, which still cling to her arm, immobile. "And I bet you know all about butterflies too, just like your sea cucumbers."

"Well, since you asked. You see, they're a fascinating representation of the cycle of life." He leaned down closer to Sophie's arm and the butterfly. "You probably learned in school about metamorphosis—how caterpillars transform into butterflies."

"I think I was out that day."

"Well, monarch butterflies rely heavily on milkweed plants for their survival and life cycle. Caterpillars feed on milkweed, which makes them poisonous to predators due to the toxins found in the plant. Monarchs lay their eggs on milkweed leaves, which then hatch into larvae. The larvae feed on milkweed and develop into caterpillars. The caterpillar transforms into a pupa, which is an inactive stage between larva and adult, and then the butterfly emerges from the pupa." He straightened up and smiled, as if waiting for applause after a presentation. After no response, he continued, "It all makes you wonder, doesn't it? About God's master plan."

"Oh, yeah. Well, I'm not really into God."

"But you do have to wonder. The complex cycle of life is, I think, fascinating."

Sophie looked back at the monarch still seated comfortably on her arm, before looking up and scanning her surroundings. "Don't you ever miss stuff? I mean, being stuck out here."

"Miss stuff? Stuck? Heck, most of the great stuff *is* right here. Observing it all, you know, that cycle I was—"

"No, I mean friends and stuff. It's just, well, it seems messed up, a waste maybe, being out here alone and all and being a kinda—". Sophie stopped, realizing she'd been staring at Cary's bare chest, and looked down. After hearing no response, she looked at him. He'd widened his eyes, cocked his head, and was giving her that sweet questioning smile that she'd seen earlier.

"Being a kind of a what?"

"I don't know…a kinda, well, cute, smart guy, I suppose." There. She said it. Embarrassed though, she wanted to change the subject, fill the silent space that followed. She looked away, then lifted her arm that held the butterfly. She gently touched one of its wings. "Look, it's not afraid!" she said. "Why wouldn't it be afraid of something so much bigger than itself?"

"They're actually social animals," Cary said. "They crave companionship. Bond easily with humans." He leaned the hoe against the shack.

"So, then, you're *not* like a butterfly," Sophie said.

"A lot bigger. Not as colorful. And I can't fly."

"No, I mean you're not a social animal. Don't crave companionship."

"It's not that." Cary looked down at his feet, bent over, picked up and examined the marks on a jagged stone before continuing. "You know, there's a great quote: 'Look deep into nature, and then you will understand everything better.' You know who said that?"

"No, but I'm no Einstein," Sophie said.

"But it *was* Einstein!" Cary said, smiling. "You nailed it!" There was a long pause, an awkward silence while they both stared at the butterfly. "Hey, where's your mom, anyway," Cary said finally.

Sophie looked up at him. Shook her head. "Oh my God, you wouldn't believe it."

"Well, try me."

"It's *so* weird. She was trying to show me something on the other side of the island." Sophie gazed back into the fog. "Wouldn't tell me what. Got really serious. I think something happened to her on the other side of the island, like a zillion years ago."

"Huh," Cary said, puzzled.

"My mom was actually here the year before I was born; here with her grandfather."

Cary followed Sophie's gaze. "When? In the '60s?

"I guess; I was born in '68."

"That's about when that fishing family lived alone out here. Anyway, that's what I heard from this land surveyor guy who came out here last month. It seems some couple set up camp here in the '60s when the island was uninhabited. They kind of homesteaded. Or squatted, really. Lived on some old sailboat most of the year at first. Even had a baby. Then they moved to the old stone house down here by the wharf." Cary pointed. "It's over there. Roof's fallen in. Also, there was a cabin someone built on the other side of the island.

Cabin's gone now, pretty much. I've seen it; just a collapsed roof sitting in a stone foundation."

Sophie looked at Cary. "So, what happened to them?"

Cary shrugged. "Beats me. The guy didn't say. Or he didn't know." He looked at Sophie and scratched his head. "He did say that one other time years ago he'd come out here, to do a land survey for the mainland family that owned Gadus, and he only saw one person on the island—a teenager." Cary paused, rubbed a finger across his lower lip. "Huh, maybe that was the baby all grown up. Anyway, the surveyor tried to talk to him, but every time he approached, the kid would run away. Disappear. Like a ghost. He told me the locals called the kid Tarzan."

Sophie looked at Cary. "So, what happened to him?"

"No idea. He's sure not here now. Unless he's one of the ghosts. Anyway, sounds like a strange dude."

Sophie smirked. "Kind of like you then, right? Out here all alone and all. She glanced at his shirtless body. Maybe I should call *you* Tarzan."

"Fine. Then you'd have to be Jane."

Sophie backed away a step. "Well, let's not make a couple thing out of this, okay? There's only three people on this island. And two will be leaving soon."

Cary was hurt. She could see that. "Well then, if I'm not Tarzan, there's that other name you gave me, the one I heard when I was rowing away in the fog yesterday. I think it was 'Total Nerd'."

Sophie flushed. "Oh. I was just—"

"Voices carry in the fog."

"I was just—"

"Careful then," Cary said. "Maybe I'm crazy like that kid who once lived out here. Or maybe I'm one of those ghosts I mentioned yesterday."

"Not that I really want to know, but what's the deal with the ghosts?"

"There's three. Well, two and a dog."

"A ghost dog?"

"Sure, dogs can be ghosts. Why not? Anyway, the story I heard is that back in the seventeenth century during the Indian Wars, Gadus was owned by one guy, a ship captain, and his island had a bunch of inhabitants. The captain was out fishing one day with his dog when he was attacked by some Native Americans who lived in the area. He was beheaded and his body was tossed overboard. His faithful dog jumped in after him. Their bodies washed up on the shore of Gadus. People say they still walk the island together to this very day, and when the fog comes in over Gadus you can sometimes catch a glimpse of the captain and his dog wandering the island."

"Creepy. Have you seen them?"

"I try not to think about it."

"Who's the other ghost?"

"That kid."

"What!? Wait a minute. He couldn't be dead; he'd still be pretty young. Like around my mom's age."

Cary put down the stone he'd picked up earlier. "Yeah, well—"

"Don't tell me he's a ghost who's wandering around too?"

Cary shrugged. They were silent for some time, staring out into the fog, until Cary suggested to Sophie that maybe her mom had gotten in trouble, fell or got lost, and maybe they should search for her. "Just a thought," he said. "And I didn't mean to creep you out about the ghosts."

"Ghosts are bullshit. And my mom can take care of herself."

"I know. I mean, I could sense that from talking with her yesterday, but still, if I were you—"

Sophie turned to him. "Well, you're not me. Okay?"

Cary stood; raised both hands as if in surrender. "Okay," he said. He turned to walk towards the wharf. After a few steps he stopped and turned back to her. "What are you so angry about, anyway?"

She took in his look, surprised that it wasn't an angry one, but one that was more soulful, genuine, and concerned. "It's a lot of stuff. Fucked up family stuff."

"Like what?"

Sophie reached down and pulled at a clump of the long grass that brushed against her ankle. "It's crazy. My parents are so different. Like it's a total mismatch or something. Fighting like a couple of hens. Yet they've been together forever. Until now, anyway. And me, I'm in the middle all the time." Sophie closed her eyes. Shook her head. Then she looked up at Cary, with hurt in her eyes. "Anyway, you wouldn't understand."

Cary walked back slowly to Sophie. Nodded slightly. "Been there. I can relate."

"Really? You seem…I mean, like you have it together."

"Ha! A minute ago, you thought I was a weird nerd living out here all alone and liking it." Cary looked down, kicked the toe of one of his rubber boots into a half buried stone.

"Well?" Sophie asked.

"Well, it's better out here. That's all. "

Sophie chuckled.

"That's funny?"

"I was just thinking. You and that crazy kid would have made a great team, roaming the island together, and catching sea cucumbers, and—"

Cary turned abruptly and began to walk back toward the wharf. "Say hi to your mom for me. I need to get some stuff done," he muttered.

Sophie watched as the fog slowly swallowed him. Mad at herself for what she had quipped and for driving him away, she put her hands on her face and sobbed.

* * *

When Cleo stepped out of the museum shack and turned north, she followed the faint path into the center part of the island. As she hiked, she asked herself, 'So, what are you doing now that Sophie isn't coming along? What is this going to accomplish, walking away, leaving behind an even more confused daughter? Still, something pulled Cleo on, and she worked her way along the path, moving faster, the grasses, rushes and the sedges with their triangular stems lightly scraping her bare legs as if naggingly questioning her as she strode through them. So, what do you expect to find from the memories? she thought. Why walk back here, back into that?

She didn't see part of an old stone foundation until she stumbled on it, her foot catching a piece of moss-covered wall, forcing her into a falling roll and onto a patch of pasture roses, their alluringly pretty pink flowers hiding stems covered with numerous hooked prickles. Cleo rose quickly, dusted herself off, and looked around at the remains of the houses' foundations. She knew about them, had explored them years before, imagining the daily lives of the people in these settlements from the 17th, 18th, and 19th centuries. Each settlement and each era had ended, Poppy had told her—some suddenly, some gradually—the people disappearing for a variety of reasons: economic, sickness, political and even weather. And of course, way back, before the foundations, were the Red Paint People. They too had disappeared. No one knew why.

Cleo was headed for the cliff. The path meandered past the freshwater wetland in the center of the island. Her nose picked up its sulfur smell. She was surprised she remembered it so clearly. She looked out at the open, rolling, boggy land which seemed somehow out of place on such a small island. As she moved inland, away from the coolness of the ocean, the fog began to disperse. Visibility was better now; she hoped for a decent view from the cliff. And she wondered about the cabin. Would it still be there?

The path led gradually upward, amidst a thickening growth of sedges, until there was a much steeper rise, which was laden with rock outcroppings interspersed with the dirt of the trail. Cleo leaned forward now, almost on all fours, and clawed her way up the final stretch. Her reward at the top, on the seaward side, was her own private clearing, one carpeted with ferns and long grasses, set on the edge of a cliff. Through the denser fog below she could just discern the empty, rolling sea to the east, and at the cliff's bottom she could make out a semicircular cove with a beach made of popplestones. The large pebbles, smooth and round from eons of relentless ocean surge, seemed to be calling up to her in an eerie, raucous chorus, as each swell grabbed the ones within reach and pulled them out to sea, until the next surge arrived to return them to the steep edge of the cove. Lost in thought, Cleo stood near the rotted trunk of a fallen, almost horizontal spruce tree, which must have been uprooted by a winter gale many years ago. Then she found a mossy patch of ground, sat down, leaned against the tree trunk, closed her eyes, and took herself back.

V

August 11, 1967 –
Afternoon and Evening, Day 1
Gadus Island

The girl is wheezing at the end of her frantic dash from the steps of the boy's cabin all the way to the wharf, where she finds Poppy on his knees in the tall grasses by the old wooden ladder. He's examining something in his right hand. She puts her hands on her hips and leans forward, trying to catch her breath. Poppy looks up at her.

"Are you practicing for the college track team? Or did you see a ghost? I was beginning to get worried, Cleo. You've been gone quite some time."

"Poppy, I'm glad you're still ashore. I was afraid I'd miss my ride out to *Archaic*."

"Well, I don't know what *you've* discovered, but *I* sure have something." He lifts his hand up to her. "Know what I have here?"

"Animal teeth?"

"Class Chondrichthyes."

"English, Poppy. Put it in English."

"They're from a wet scaled vertebrate."

"Poppy, in English, please. I've had a long day. Believe me."

"They're shark teeth. I found them in what I expected was a burial site."

"Why would someone bury shark teeth?"

"It could have to do with shamans. Remember when you were little and I told you about shamans?"

"The guys they thought could see beyond objects, into the spirit world."

"Yes, and these teeth may indicate the presence of shamans on this island four thousand or so years ago."

"Not following. Fish teeth equal shamans?"

"I'll explain later. But this is very, very exciting. And also…" He pauses. Looks mystified. And concerned.

"Also what, Poppy?"

"Something else."

"What?"

"Another grave."

"Well, that's exciting!"

Poppy shakes his head. "More like concerning."

"Why?"

"It's not from the period."

"You mean older that archaic?"

Poppy looks back toward the trail where Cleo had emerged. He doesn't respond.

"Poppy, what? What's up?"

"Not older," he says finally. "Younger. Much younger. Too fresh a grave to dig, in fact." He turns to Cleo. We need to stay on the island a while." Poppy groans a bit while slowly getting to his feet. "Oh, my dear, these old bones of mine are feeling it in this damp weather." He dusts off his worn khaki pants with both hands. Looks up at his granddaughter. "So, anyway, what did you find today? Something must have caught your interest. Not our odd but handsome rescuer, by any chance? I hope he at least told you his name."

"He did. It's Aiden."

Poppy chuckled. "Ah, little fire."

"What?"

"The name Aiden has roots in Irish mythology and means 'little fire'. You best be careful to not be captivated by his primordial allure."

"His what?"

"Primordial allure."

"Sounds like a beauty cream brand in some glamour magazine."

"It means primeval charm. Anyway, since you indeed did see him, I hope he was polite, properly attired, and took you out to one of the finer establishments on the island for lunch."

Cleo is torn between keeping the promise she'd made to the boy, and the value of telling Poppy about his need for help, which would surely be in all their best interests. But she decides to wait. To think on it. Maybe check on Aiden. Maybe spy on him. Tomorrow.

She smiles at her grandfather. "No, Poppy, all the better restaurants were closed. So, he took me for a ride on his elephant, showed me all the sights."

Poppy nods. Winks at her. Laughs. "You're too much. Did I ever tell you you're the best granddaughter I've ever had?"

"Poppy, I'm your *only* granddaughter."

"Still, it holds true, Ohkuk," he replies, reaching down for his shovel, trowel, spade and bucket. "Well, we should head to the boat and think about what to make for dinner. I was thinking maybe Chateaubriand with creamy steamed asparagus and saffron rice pilaf."

"So, you mean we'll be having the rest of that two day-old beef stew and more of those stale crackers."

"Exactly."

At the edge of the wharf, Poppy stops and looks at his grand-daughter. "No sense bringing the archeology tools back to the boat. The tide is down pretty far now and it's a long way down that slippery wharf ladder." He turns and scans the empty island. "This is quite a place. A naturalist's dream, really—amazing plant, sea and bird life, flush with rocky beaches, jagged cliffs, and intriguing wooded trails. But the bedrock, Ohkuk! Did you know that the geologic history recorded in this bedrock spans over half a billion years?" Lost in thought, he pauses for what appears to the girl as a very long time.

Then he nods and looks over at her. "Did you know that several major cycles of deposition, deformation, and igneous activity related to plate tectonic subduction and collision are responsible for the complex bedrock that we observe right here today."

She smiles pertly at her grandfather. "Poppy, if we don't get going that Chateaubriand of yours is going to spoil."

"No, it keeps forever."

Cleo rolls her eyes. "Believe me, I know. It's beginning to seem that way."

They work their way carefully down the slippery ladder to their skiff, and climb aboard. Poppy takes the oars. On their row out to *Archaic*, Cleo spies something at the very head of the narrow harbor. "There's a boat down there, Poppy. We must have missed it when we came ashore." Poppy turns their skiff and rows toward the boat to get a closer look. "She's an old vessel," Poppy says. "Almost abandoned. The mast is long gone, but I bet she was a stout sailing cutter in her day." He rows closer and around the stern to get a look at the hailing port. *Perseverance. New Bedford.* The old yacht is a sad sight. The boat's sides are bleeding—rust from the planks' decaying iron boat nails streaks the faded and chipped white hull. A green slime grows on her waterline, like a marine beard needing trimming. One of her portholes is covered with a delaminated piece of plywood, like a hasty patch thrown over a wounded eye. A small outboard powered lobster boat is tied on one side; on the other is a half-sunken float stacked with lobster traps. "That must be that island boy's boat," Poppy says as he edges closer. "The old sailboat must be his, too. Or his parents'. Do they live aboard? Or on the island? And where are they? It's all a bit odd." Poppy stops. Ships his oars. He seems deep in thought as the skiff drifts seaward. "You know, I keep thinking of that bayonet tucked

69

in the boy's belt. I once saw one similar in a colleague's collection at the Peabody Museum at Harvard. It may date to, or even before, the Red Paint People. And what was around his neck—I first thought they were small animal or seagull bones, but…" Poppy reaches into his pocket. "But I think some were these," he says, holding up the shark teeth. Cleo remembers now. When she was half carrying the boy, she'd had a closer look at what hung from his neck. Some *did* look like shark teeth. Poppy puts the oars back in the oarlocks and starts to row out to *Archaic*. But after a few strokes he stops again. Looks at his granddaughter. "That boy knows something. Or found something. I should talk to him."

Cleo is nervous. "Maybe not, Poppy. I mean, maybe he just wants to be left alone. You always said we should respect a person's space, so…"

Poppy starts to row again, then lifts the oars out of the water, and lets the skiff glide along from the thrust of his last stroke while closing one eye, tilting his head, and looking suspiciously at his granddaughter. But he says nothing.

* * *

That evening at dinner Cleo had been uncharacteristically quiet. She mostly stared ashore and only picked at her dinner before she stood, plate in hand, and headed into the cabin. "I'd better knock off some more of my summer reading, Poppy." She gave him a kiss on the cheek and headed to her bunk in the bow cabin of *Archaic*. She had two books left —*Lord of the Flies* and *Siddhartha*—and had been switching back and forth depending on her mood, rather than finishing one first. She took *Lord of the Flies* off the mahogany shelf by her bunk, propped two pillows against the bulkhead, turned up the lantern wick above her head, and tried to settle in. But her mind wandered. She couldn't stop thinking about Aiden. She told herself she had to go back, that she couldn't leave him there alone in his cabin, even if he wanted her to. Part of her was naturally fearful. Part of her was curious. Part of her felt she could definitely help him. And part of her realized Poppy was right about Aiden's primordial allure.

She put down *Lord of the Flies*. Picked up *Siddhartha*, opened to her bookmark, and started reading.

She drew him toward her with her eyes, he inclined his face toward hers and lay his mouth on her mouth, which was like a freshly split-open fig. For a long time he kissed Kamala, and Siddhartha was filled with deep astonishment...

Cleo closed her eyes and shook her head. Was this some sign that she had opened the book to *this* particular section? Were she and Aiden star-crossed lovers? Maybe meant to be? God, Cleo, you're such a romantic, she thought. But maybe fate *had* brought them together, two teens from different worlds—one educated and socialized in the most sophisticated of environments, the other growing up wild, a part of nature, in a wild part of the world yet, it seemed, self-educated. An island-based Thoreau. She closed the book. But something did seem very wrong with him. She'd seen that in his bizarre behavior. And he was hurt. Out there with no help. No, she decided, she'd go back tomorrow. She'd tell Poppy she was seeing him because he might give her some information about anything he'd discovered from the Red Paint People. And that, after all, was sort of the truth. Still, she thought, she had to be careful. Maybe she would only spy on him, keep her distance, just see if he's okay, and maybe drop off some food. That would work. After all, he couldn't catch her. He couldn't walk. Satisfied with her decision, she began to doze off, with

Siddhartha now leaning on her chin. Her thoughts drifted to Kamala and Siddhartha, with their open mouths coming together. She felt a rising warmth between her thighs, and pressed her legs together, either to feel it stronger or not let it get away. And as she entered that intangible twilight zone between consciousness and sleep, her mind's final image was the radiant brown and green of Aiden's piercing eyes.

VI

August 12, 1967 – Day 2
Gadus Island

After breakfast the next morning, as he finished putting away the morning's coffee mugs and plates, Poppy began singing an old Irving Taylor tune in his Dean Martin voice.

Everybody loves somebody sometime
Everybody falls in love somehow

Everybody finds somebody someplace
Something in my heart keeps saying
My someplace is here

Cleo cocked her head. Looked down from her perch in the cockpit. "Poppy, are you looking for love? 'Cause as far as I can tell, except for me, there are no girls within ten miles of here." She looked ashore. "Unless there's some Red Paint hunter-gatherer chick still hiding on Gadus."

Poppy smiled. "Well, maybe it's just this special place that's the 'someplace' in the song. And maybe it's being with another love: my granddaughter."

Cleo's eyes watered. She looked down, pretending to retie her sneakers. "Poppy, did you ever want to fall in love again. I mean... you know, with another woman, like you were with Grandma?"

Poppy carefully folded the worn dishtowel and came up on deck. "No, my dear, your grandmother gave me such wonderful memories. I think that should be enough to last to the end. Even in the hardest times, after your mother's..." Poppy looked away, wiped his eyes. "Some people get lucky with love. And if that love is strong enough, it won't ever go away. Even when the loved ones do."

They both were silent for a while, staring toward shore. "Poppy, about my dad. I mean, what's with that? It doesn't ever seem—well, even when Mom was sick—that he was ever like you and Grandma, being so, you know, caring and working together. Dad's so—"

Poppy interrupted his granddaughter. "It's hard to understand." He shook his head. "They did get married quite young, first year in college in fact. They felt they should, I guess. And you came right along that spring. So, maybe they were never in love. I don't know. I thought I would understand by now about your father. Yes, he became a widower, but didn't seem to act that way." Poppy closed his eyes, then opened them and gazed seaward. "But your grandma and I lost our *child*. Your mother." Poppy shook his head, the look on his face the saddest Cleo had seen in many years. "There's no word for that, you know," he continued. "You lose your husband, you're a widow; lose your wife, you're a widower; lose parents as a child, you're an orphan." His voice choked, but he continued, "Yet we have no word for when the parent loses a child. There can't be, it's too painful to be a word." Cleo leaned on Poppy's shoulder. He continued. "When you've had great loss, the word 'precious' takes on a whole new meaning; you don't ever again waste a single moment because you know that things can...well, anyway, back to your dad. I thought maybe, at my advanced age, I'd have the wisdom to see where things went awry with him." He paused. "I could speculate, I suppose. Sometimes, it's not love, but just a series of circumstances that push people together. The best thing I can do now is to make things the best I can for you; help you keep growing as the compassionate, bright and curious child you've always been." Poppy looked toward the island; a gull appeared to be limping, struggling somehow, at water's edge along the mudflats. "You were always the child that tried to save the wounded bird," he said. "And sometimes that didn't work, but I guess you had to try." He changed his gaze to the wharf; the fast departing tide had exposed the depth of the wharf's foundation. "I'll always try to make things the best for you, despite your dad, until the tide goes out for me. Then, well...I guess you'll be on your own." He shook his head again. Cleo saw a hint of anger come to his eyes. "It does hurt that after your mother...well, anyway, since then your father really doesn't seem very involved, and he certainly doesn't want to give me a very long leash with you." He thought for a moment. "Or give my anchor more scope with you, which would be the proper metaphor, I guess." He looked over at his granddaughter. "At least he didn't stop you from coming on this trip." He put his hand on her arm. "But enough metaphors. We'll both be fine. We're safe here together. I think there's plenty of water under us."

Cleo tried to cover up her emotion. "Is that another metaphor? Or are you just worried about this low tide?"

Poppy chuckled. "Good one, Ohkuk."

Cleo felt a sudden pang of guilt, knowing she had planned to keep something from her grandfather, and even tell a lie—well, really just a white lie. But then Poppy spoke again.

"Cleo, do you remember when you were little, and I told you about red ocher during one of our Archeology Saturdays on my porch? How the bones in graves were buried with red ocher? And how, because of this, in 1913 an archeologist named Warren Moorehead named these people the Red Paint People. Anyway, some sites have been found with slate bayonets and other artifacts, also covered in red ocher. I know I mentioned it before, but I'm getting increasingly fascinated by what looked like a bayonet in that boy's belt, and if it is, what he may know or lead us to."

Cleo became anxious. "Poppy, I told you that I don't think he..."

"Yes, but maybe, if you're diplomatic, and happen to see him again, well…"

Cleo was relieved. She wouldn't have to come up with an excuse or white lie about seeing Aiden.

"Okay. That's fine, Poppy."

"And if you see him, do find out about the whereabouts of his parents. Seems odd they're not around."

"Okay. And what will you be doing?"

"I'll be in the shell middens. Digging." Poppy looked ashore. "You know, Cleo, with my digging, coupled with what you might learn from that boy, well, it could be a big day for us and archeology!"

* * *

Later that morning, on the hike back to Aiden's cabin, Cleo stopped several times, uncertain about what she was doing. Once, she even turned around and walked back a few yards before taking a deep breath, turning, and resuming her route. As she got closer, she mulled over her options: should she just announce herself and say that she had come back only to drop off food? Or should she sneak up to the window, peak in, and just drop off the food she'd gathered for him, then quietly back away. She decided on that plan.

When she got to the grove of trees within sight of the cabin, she ducked behind one of the spruces, and listened. The only sound was the distant surf and the gentle swish of the tree limbs. The branches, which opened and closed with the breeze, let the late morning sun send intermittent shafts of light into the grove and against the side of the cabin. She moved forward, quietly and slowly through the tramped down tufts of encroaching grasses along the path. She crept to the cabin's windowless back side, flattened herself against the wall, and took a few deep breaths before slowly working her way along the wall to the front side. As she crouched beneath the half-opened window, she felt a wave of panic; she took more deep breaths, and suppressed the urge to turn and run. Then she stood, ever so slowly, and peeked in the window. He was there, half turned away from her, seemingly engrossed in a book, and sitting in one of the handmade log and sapling chairs she'd seen earlier. His bad ankle, propped up on the lobster trap table, was wrapped with what looked like the torn-off arm of a sweatshirt. As Cleo stared at Aiden, trying to decide whether to knock on the window, his voice startled her.

"I told you not to come. And still you came," he said, not looking up from the book.

Cleo hesitated. "I was just…how did you know…"

"The shadows told me. You stopped the morning sun when you stood in the window. So, the shadows told me. Others told me, too. That you were coming."

"Who?"

No answer.

"I brought you food, that's all. Food and an ace bandage from our medical kit. How is your ankle?"

"You were to leave the island."

Cleo backed away from the window. "Tomorrow. I think we're leaving tomorrow. I'll leave the food and bandage on the stoop." She bent down to pick up her bag. It's done, she thought. I'm not his nursemaid for God's sake. I've done enough. As she picked up the bag, she thought she heard him speak. She stood and glanced in. He had turned, and was looking straight at her. A shaft of morning sunlight ran across the rough wooden floor of the cabin to where he sat, illuminating him as he stared at her. The light seemed to dance in his eyes for just a moment, until the spruce branches closed again when the wind lulled, shutting out the sun. "I had asked you, 'Which is better, law and rescue, or hunting and breaking things up?'"

Cleo stared back, confused. Then Aiden lifted the opened book skyward, like a priest delivering communion. "It's from *Lord of the Flies*. It's Piggy. Piggy's last words," he said.

Cleo is suddenly not confused, and also amazed and somehow less fearful. "You won't believe this, but I'm reading that book right now. It's on the boat."

"Why would I not believe you?"

"I don't know. Kind of an amazing coincidence. It's part of my summer reading to prepare for my first year at college. I'm almost at the end. Chapter 10."

"So, is it the law that you rescue me? Or should I continue to hunt and break things up?"

"Hunt? Hunt for what? I don't understand."

"No. You must go."

Cleo, bag still in hand, angrily stomped away from the window and around to the door, pushed it open, stepped into the cabin, and stared at him. "What about kindness? Did anyone ever teach you about kindness?" She held up the bag with the food and bandage. "*This* is kindness, asshole. Okay?"

Aiden froze, then curled up, almost into himself, head in hands. Cleo didn't move. Said nothing. Finally, she spoke. "I'm…I'm sorry. I didn't mean to…"

He looked up at her, a mixture of hurt and yearning on his face, but said nothing.

"Could I come back tomorrow? Before I leave. I'll read those last two chapters. We can talk."

Aiden nodded. Three times.

Cleo put down the bag, turned to the door, and walked down the three steps. This time she didn't run, but walked slowly along the path, thinking about a book. It wasn't *Lord of the Flies*. It was *Siddhartha*.

* * *

When Cleo emerged from the inland trail, she scanned the wharf area for Poppy. He was nowhere to be seen. She headed over to the spot on the southeast side of the island near a small freshwater stream; it was where he'd said he'd be digging in the shell middens. She found remnants of his dig, but no Poppy, so she went back to the wharf to wait for him to appear. It occurred to her on the way that maybe he had returned to *Archaic* to retrieve something. Sure enough, their skiff was tied astern of the old sloop. She could just make out the shape of what had to be Poppy sitting in the cockpit. She yelled and waved. She cupped her hands and yelled louder. POPEEEEEE! Her voice echoed off the high granite shore on the harbor's opposite side. Still no response. And no movement. Suddenly worried that he'd had a heart attack or stroke, she fought back panic. Over the next ten minutes she paced back and forth along the wharf, yelling his name, while trying to think of a way to get out to him. There was only one option: to swim. She knew she wouldn't be able to pull herself up *Archaic*'s high sides, but she could pull herself up and into the skiff, then pull the skiff in and climb aboard the big boat. And it wasn't too long a swim. She knew Maine waters were cold, even in August, but she was a strong swimmer and was confident she could make it before her muscles cramped. She moved to the edge of the wharf, pulled off her sneakers, yanked the heavy belt off of her cutoff jean shorts, tightened the front knot of her red halter top, and descended the rickety, slimy ladder. At the last step she pushed off. She was assaulted by cold water shock, the blood vessels in her skin closing, her heart working dramatically harder, her breathing becoming rapid. Still, she swam a fast crawl, resisting the urge to turn around to the ladder, focusing only on *Archaic*'s mast each time she turned up her head for a breath. But her pace gradually became slower and more ragged, and, like a tiring runner, her muscles lost power, her limbs felt slow and heavy, her head became dizzy, and her mind disoriented. Her arms, now almost flailing, barely propelled her forward. Still, the mast she focused on seemed to get closer. And then she was there! Her right arm flopped over the skiff's rail, and, with a supreme effort, she rolled herself into the small boat, nearly submerging the rail in the process. She lay there on her back, wheezing and coughing, her chest tight, staring at the bright blue, cloudless sky until her breath returned. Then she sat up, moved forward to the skiff's bow line, pulled herself up to *Archaic*, and looked over the sloop's stern. Poppy was leaning against the cabin bulkhead, a book in his lap, snoring loudly. Cleo climbed aboard and stood over him, dripping. "POPEEEE!" He opened his eyes, furrowed his brow. "My my, you're soaking wet, Ohkuk. This water is much too cold for swimming."

"POPPY, YOU TOTALLY FREAKED ME OUT. I thought you'd died."

"My dear, when that time comes, I'll be sure to tell you, for goodness' sake. Now please get some dry clothes on before you shiver so hard your teeth fall out." Cleo headed down the cabin steps. "And Cleo," Poppy continued, "thank you." Cleo turned; a questioning look was on her face. She saw wetness in her grandfather's eyes. "Thanks for what, Poppy?"

"For caring so much."

An hour later Cleo emerged from the forward cabin dressed in her pink and white "Make Love Not War" sweatshirt and bell-bottom jeans embroidered with flowers. Poppy, hunched over a frying pan and saucepan on the old stove, looked up, shook his head and smiled. "You must be planning to head to that big love fest on Gadus Island."

"Ha ha. What's for dinner, Poppy?"

"Deux repas, mon chéri! This evening we will be serving two of the tastiest offerings of fine cuisine ever to come from a can: Boyardee Beefaroni with a side of B&M Brown Bread."

"Okay. As long as you're sure that these cans aren't from the Paleolithic period."

"Not a chance, Ohkuk. For us, strictly Neolithic New Stone Age cuisine."

"Then let's dig in soon, professor. I'm starved."

"I found your digging spot when I came out of the trail and looked for you this afternoon. Poppy," Cleo said during dinner. "How do you know what spot to even start at?"

"Well, Ohkuk, I have learned to follow a strict set of criteria: the best spots in Maine are in sheltered coves or bays, near tidal flats and often near tidal or inland streams. They usually face south and east. Another good spot can be a more exposed, seaward-facing bluff or beach. These sites may be the result of periodic consumption of large amounts of shellfish and/or long continuous occupation, or may represent seasonal gatherings."

"So why would bones be there, in those spots?"

"In the climate of Maine, buried bones quickly dissolve in acid soils, but in shell middens, bones are preserved by the calcium carbonate of the mollusk shells that make up most of the midden. Bones of animals, fish, and even swordfish can be preserved. This bone tells archaeologists what animals were important to the site's inhabitants. The midden can also contain fragments of pottery and even house floors and fire hearths."

"Swordfish?"

"This was a swordfish hunting culture, the earliest in the entire world. The remains of many swordfish have been found in middens, along with the tools used to hunt them. Other animals important to the sites' occupants included cod, moose, deer, bear and beaver."

"What about human bones?"

"Yes. But whether the placement of human remains into shell middens might be the result of taphonomic processes or deliberate human action we're not sure."

"Taphonomic?"

"The study of how organic remains pass from the biosphere to the lithosphere."

"English, Poppy. Say it in ENGLISH."

"That's the process affecting remains from the time of death of an organism through decomposition, burial, and preservation as mineralized fossils or other stable biomaterials. There has been a surprising lack of research into the reason for this phenomenon. Traditional studies of middens have often interpreted the human bones as discarded waste, remnants of cannibalistic practices or disturbed burials. A small number of studies have discovered more complex social and ritual reasons for the placement of bones into the shell middens."

"Cannibals! Sorry I asked."

Poppy smiled and handed her a dishtowel. "Anyway, dear one, no great discoveries on my end today. But what did *you* discover before you decided to jump into this 50 degree water?"

"Well, the island boy lives in this weird cabin on the other side of the island. Actually, it's kind of half a cabin. I can't explain it. But inside it's full of books. I mean, Poppy, even more books than you have in your study back home. And he uses big words. So, I think they're his books. He was reading when I saw him. Oh, and his furniture! It's all handmade of twigs and branches. Even his bed."

"A weird half cabin, filled with books, and furnished with furniture made of sticks. This sounds like a fairy tale. Did you smoke something when you put on those hippy clothes, my dear?"

"Poppy, it's no fairy tale. Hardly."

"Did you ask about his parents?"

"He wouldn't answer about where his parents are, but said there were 'others' with him."

"Others? There's no one else on this island, as far as I can tell."

"Poppy, this is weird, but it seems, sometimes, well, that he talks to—well, kind of nods at—people who aren't there."

Poppy slid the saucepan and frying pan into the cabinet under the stove. Then he sat on the starboard bunk. She could tell he was thinking deep thoughts. Finally, he spoke. "If he's been alone for some time, a significantly long period of time, he may be creating company. Imaginary company. We all need companionship. Someone to care for us. Someone to care for. Maybe he doesn't have that. It is strange though, if he is indeed alone, how that came to be. I'm no doctor, and I'm not saying this is it, but with that kind of behavior…well, it's possible it could be early onset of schizophrenia."

"God. That's scary. Maybe…God, I don't know, Poppy…It all just seems so sad."

"Being the one cared for is one thing, but sometimes I think that caring *for* someone is really what humanity is all about." Poppy stood up slowly, rubbed the small of his back, and looked out the main hatch toward shore, just as a pair of Common Eider ducks flew over them and landed next to the skiff tied astern. Cleo stood next to her grandfather and they both stared out the hatch.

"Those are pretty. Do you think they're a couple, Poppy?"

"Could be. Speaking of caring, those eiders are very caring birds. Did you know that young Common Eiders often benefit from the care of "aunts," which are nonbreeding females. These "aunts" gather around nests containing hatching eggs or newly hatched young and accompany the ducklings to the water with their mother and help to protect the young from predators. Also, I've heard that in very cold conditions some eiders will move around the outer ring of the flock in order to keep the water from freezing on the others. Now, that's caring for someone!"

Cleo nodded. "Like the way you did with Grandma when she was in bed all that time with emphysema." She looked over at her grandfather with a mixture of awe and respect. "God, Poppy, those three years, picking Grandma up to change sheets, spoon feeding her, even changing her diaper, and I never once heard you complain!"

"Well, everyone has their own responsibilities and burdens. Caring is part of being. A big part. Don't ever forget that."

"I guess so, but…"

"Think about it, Cleo. Life begins with caring and ends with caring. A baby at first is totally helpless, can't walk or get their own food, so someone has to care. Then, in old age—or, sadly, even before then with some—it happens again. They often can't walk, can't even feed themselves at that point. Just like babies. Full cycle."

"Well, *you* won't get that way."

Poppy looked out at the pair of eiders. Said nothing.

"Well, right now I'm saddled with the burden of finishing my summer reading. Two more chapters of *Lord of the Flies*, Poppy, and I'm done for the summer!"

Poppy looked ashore. "Ah, *Lord of the Flies*. Civilization versus savagery. I wonder: who is that boy living here on Gadus Island? Is he a Ralph or is he a Jack?"

"Oh my God, Poppy, you've read the book! You never told me."

"I figured we'd discuss it when you were done. As for those last two chapters, well, hang onto your hat!"

VII

August 13, 1967
Gadus Island – Day 3

The day dawned clear and windless, and they sat silently, side by side in the cockpit, occasionally scanning the horizon between spoonfuls of Grape-Nuts cereal topped with generous doses of wild blueberries. They'd picked the berries a few days earlier on one of the islands to the west of Gadus, and had been joyous about their bounty as they headed down the hill back to the skiff. Then Poppy slipped and fell while carrying his bucket. She'd hurried over to help him. He seemed fine, though, standing slowly, dusting himself off, reaching down for his bucket and then beginning to pick up the spilled berries. But it had disturbed Cleo, perhaps because for the first time in her young life she'd realized how fragile—and finite— life really was.

Now, she put down her cereal bowl and looked at her grandfather. "Are you headed back to that same digging spot today, Poppy?"

"I think so. I just have a feeling…well, we'll see."

"Okay. Just don't leave me stranded ashore this time."

"Oh. You'd rather not take another brisk swim to get back to the boat?"

"Poppy, I'm *still* shivering from that!"

"Cleo, I've been thinking. Maybe you should help me in the middens today. There's something about that boy that—"

"Poppy, it's just that, well, it's just that I made him a promise."

"Oh, dear! A promise?"

"A book. Remember that I told you how much he reads? Well, he really wants to read a book I mentioned. So, I said I'd bring it to him." Cleo flushed a bit. Well, she thought, it's sort of the truth.

"All the way to the other side of the island to bring him a book?"

"And some food." She'd blurted that out without thinking.

"Some food? So that's where two of those Beefaroni cans went yesterday. Why on earth does he need food? He *lives* here, for goodness' sake. He must have *food*."

"He does somewhere, I guess. But he might run out. You see, it's his foot, Poppy. His ankle. He sprained it. So, he needs help."

Poppy smiled. "You know, my dear, you have always had a wonderful blend of curiosity and compassion."

"Thank you, Poppy."

"I'm not done. But you also love big challenges: first to volunteer for some hefty school project that the others shy away from, first to volunteer to speak to that school bully, first to—."

"What's wrong with that?"

"It's admirable, but it also puts you on the front line."

"That's how great things get done. On the front line."

"I suppose," Poppy said, shaking his head, but he was thinking: *that's also where you get shot.* He continued, "Cleo, if you want to help him, what you really need to do is to find out about his parents. Promise me you'll find out this time."

"Okay, Poppy. I promise." She stood, picking up her cereal bowl. "I'm going forward to my cabin to get my backpack."

"And don't wear that Free Love outfit."

* * *

They had planned on getting an early start before the day heated up. At 7:30 Cleo pulled the skiff up to *Archaic's* stern and effortlessly slid herself over the sloop's rail and into the small rowboat. She carefully held it alongside and waited for her grandfather, who was rummaging around in the cabin for a piece of equipment. "I'll row in, Poppy," she said when he finally appeared on deck. He carefully lowered himself into the skiff, sitting in the stern, facing his granddaughter. He was wearing his characteristic floppy canvas hat, worn canvas pants, and an old white dress shirt with the sleeves rolled up. As they rowed in Poppy smirked slightly, looked away, then rolled his eyes. Cleo, despite straining at the oars, noticed this. "What? It's these pants, isn't it? I'm just wearing them again because I don't—"

"No, the pants are fine, I guess."

"This then?" She gestured to her sleeveless maroon ringer tank top.

Poppy was embarrassed. It was the tiniest of tops, and she was clearly braless. But he couldn't bring himself to say that. So, he just looked ashore.

"It's going to be hot today, Poppy. And it's a long hike. So, this is suitable."

"Perhaps not the demurest, that's all." It was the most a grandfather could say.

* * *

It was hotter than she had expected on the hike up to Aiden's cabin, especially when weighed down with a knapsack filled with canned food and three books. Cleo's stomach was filled also—filled with butterflies. Her mind was swirling with thoughts of how Aiden would react to her on this third visit. She thought of what her friend Chloe always said about the third time with a boy. Cleo shook it off as silly.

At the grove of trees near the cabin, as she had the day prior, she stopped and listened. It was quieter and darker than before; the overhanging tree branches, immobile on this windless morning, locked out the sun. Cleo decided that this time she would announce herself. It seemed appropriate. No more sneaking around. She swallowed. Took a breath. "Aiden. Aiden. It's Cleo. I'm back. With books. And food." There was no response. She moved closer. "Aiden? Hello." The only sound was the occasional "cheep cheep cheep" of an Osprey, coming from high above in one of treetops. Otherwise, all was quiet. She stood for a while before deciding to approach the cabin and knock on the rusty screen door. She went up the three steps and looked in before knocking. The cabin appeared empty. Tentatively, she knocked. No response. She stood still and listened; hearing nothing, she reached for the door handle and opened it slowly, remembering the squeak it had made the day before. She went in. "Hello. Aiden? Okay if I come in?" She moved to the center of the cabin and stood by the crude table, which appeared to be made of four planks of driftwood. A book was open upside down on the table, along with a ring-bound writing journal. The open page was filled with a neat cursive. Cleo hesitated, looked around, then leaned down over the journal, and began reading:

I've been watching you, Osprey
And you watch me,
But neither of us prey on the other
And so, we stare, wondering how and why we do what we do—
You: spotting fish from 100 feet above,
Diving and plucking your prey, then flying away
To treetop nest to feed your mate and chicks
While keeping watch for the hungry circling eagle,
And maybe, sometimes looking down at me, alone,
You wonder, perhaps, why I, unlike you, don't mate for life
Or mate at all

And maybe you wonder too, who is my prey?
My prey that held her screaming in rough hands
Held the one who mated once for me,
To give me life. And love.

I know you, my prey
And I know you fear I do,
You, the one now left from two
So, fear my spear
Osprey talon-sharp for you
It's what will carry you away, my prey.

Cleo straightened. Her mind raced. Her eyes darted from one corner of the cabin to the other. Balanced on the edge of flight, she backed a half step. She heard a light chopping, then a rhythmic tapping, coming from behind the cabin. The chopping started again, then stopped. She turned for the door. Standing in front of her was Aiden. He held a walking stick made from what looked like a birch branch. He was staring at her, a shiny chisel and a wooden mallet clasped tightly in one hand.

Her heart jumped. "I called out for you. No answer. So...so I came in," Cleo said. She tried to read his eyes, to sense his reaction to finding her in his cabin, but the morning light behind him was silhouetting only his frame in the door.

"Was back in the lean-to. Getting a different one, a sharper one." He held up the chisel.

"Took a while to get it, with this foot and all," he said, looking down.

Cleo, wide-eyed, stepped backward. "Please don't—"

He cocked his head, then gave her just a hint of a smile. "For my decoys. The chisel is for carving my duck decoys."

"Oh. I thought—"

"Common Eiders usually. And Wood Ducks. My best. I keep some for myself. Sell some, too, on the mainland to collectors when I go in to sell my catch and buy food."

Cleo was encouraged. It was the most he'd ever said to her. She nodded and began to remove her knapsack. "Speaking of food, I brought more, and three books." Aiden worked his way over to his bed and sat down. He held up the mallet and chisel, still clasped together in one hand. "Could you take these? Put them on the table." Cleo moved tentatively to him, reached out for the carving tools, backed away quickly and placed them on the table next to the journal. Aiden watched her carefully. "Did you read them?"

"Read them?" She thought of what she'd just read in his journal on the table. It made her fearful again. "Well, I—"

"The last two chapters. Did you read the last two chapters?"

"Oh. *Lord of the Flies*. Yes. Of course."

"Tell me then. Tell me what you think."

"What I think? Well– It's just so sad in the end. Sad about Piggy. And Simon. Dying and all."

"People die," Aiden said. His face took on that distant look she'd seen before. She was scared again. She wanted to move on. But Aiden continued. "In the book Ralph almost died, too. Not Jack, though."

"I'm sad for Ralph, too, of course."

"You like Ralph?"

"Well, I guess I'd be on his team, if I were a little kid stuck on an island with no adults."

"Why? Because he's not evil? Is it that simple: Ralph is good. Simon is good. Piggy is good. And Jack is bad? Do you think that? That it's black and white."

He was challenging her, a girl who had never been afraid of a challenge. Her fear began to evaporate. She looked down for a moment to gather her thoughts. "There's evil everywhere, you know. Like in Vietnam right now. And even on those supposed island paradises."

"It's not the islands' fault," he said.

"But in this book, how can children turn so quickly into murderous savages and then, suddenly, on the beach in front of that Navy officer from the ship that finally finds them, they turn right back into scared children? I mean, is it because this fancy uniformed officer from the adult world snaps them back into being children?"

Aiden looked straight at Cleo. He seemed unfocused now. Or lost. Or distracted, somehow. She waited for his response. Instead, he abruptly turned to the door and nodded at something. Then he shook his head. Then he nodded again. Cleo was confused. "I don't...I don't understand...*who* are you nodding at?"

He turned back to her. "Would you like to see my decoys?" It was as if someone had thrown a switch, told him to move on, turn the page.

Cleo looked at him questioningly, then nodded.

"They're in that big wooden box behind the door."

She walked over, lifted the lid of the handmade box, and looked inside at a half dozen decoys. "Oh, my! They're beautiful."

"Pull one out."

She carefully lifted out the most striking one. It was a work of art, extravagantly carved and colored—the body and feathers a combination of iridescent greens, blues, tan, and chestnut. The decoy's bold white chin strap and facial stripes added to its distinctive beauty. She held it higher, up to the light. "You carved this? It's so real. So magnificent. Even the eyes. God, they stare right at me."

"It's a Wood Duck. The eyes are glass."

"So beautiful. A female, no doubt."

"No, a male. The females are less colorful."

Cleo smirked. "Well, that's not right."

Aiden furrowed his brow.

Cleo continued. "Where did you learn to do this? Did your parents—"

He reached back over his ears behind his head, gathered his long black hair and twisted it forcefully several times. "I have no parents. Only my people," he said blankly.

"Your people?" Cleo looked around the room. With one arm she made a sweeping gesture. "Where are these people that you talk about and, well, seem to look at? Aiden, I don't understand you. Please. Just tell me. What happened to your parents?"

Aiden focused on her. His blank look was gone now. In its place was a face of intense yearning. "I wish to touch you again," he said.

Cleo stepped back. Before her was a mysterious, intriguing, complicated, and perhaps delusional young man. But also, here was an imposing person of strength, adroitness, even gracefulness. She stood still. Stared at him. Several long strands of his black, shoulder length hair hung down over his thick eyebrows, falling over both sides of his straight nose. The ends of the strands brushed the top of his lips, lips that were almost feminine.

"Touch me again? What are you—"

"Yes. Like on the hill. When I fell."

Cleo backed away again, glanced at the open door, and then told herself that it was okay—he couldn't run. He could barely walk. "Well…I mean, you can't just *do* that," she said, finally. She realized Aiden's eyes were now on the decoy that she cradled in her arms like a baby.

"Why? You have the same beauty as what I made there, there in what you are holding. I asked you to hold it. And you are holding it. You held me before. On the hill. You can let me hold you now."

Cleo glanced down at the beautiful, smooth, colorful body of the decoy. She shook her head. "This is freaking me out." She turned toward the door. No, she thought, I'm not walking out of this. She turned back to him. "Aiden, it doesn't work that way in my world. In my world you need to share first, before—"

"You can have one of my decoys then." He nodded to the Wood Duck in her arms. "That one if you want."

"No, no. That's not it. You, well, *we* need to talk. That's how I mean share. Look, I'm glad to tell you anything you want to know about me, if then you tell me something about you. Fair is fair."

As if searching for approval, he looked back to the spot by the door where he'd gestured at something earlier, then shrugged, and looked back at Cleo.

She continued. "Look, I have an idea. We'll do one fact each about us, even if it's a little one. One at a time. Taking turns." She smiled at him. "And I'll even start." She didn't wait for a response. "Okay, I was born in Marblehead, Massachusetts." She stopped. Nodded. "There. Now, you go."

Aiden spent some time taking this in before saying, "Here."

"Here? You were born *here*?"

"Yes."

"Okay, I guess. But really? Way out here on this island? No hospital or doctor?"

Aiden nodded.

"So, was that because—" Cleo began.

Aiden interrupted. "No. It's your turn. Fair is fair."

"Okay." Cleo paused. Took a deep breath. "My mom died of cancer when I was eight."

Aiden was silent for what seemed like a few minutes, then pushed himself up from his bed, and leaned forward on his cane. He didn't speak.

"And your mom?" Cleo asked, finally.

Aiden shook his head. "No."

"Oh, so she didn't die."

"I don't know."

"You don't know? But—"

"I don't know for sure," he said. And just then something seemed to change. For the first time, his voice seemed unguarded, and Cleo sensed an almost palpable exhale, a release of some repressed feeling coming from him. She was encouraged.

"It's okay to talk. It's always okay to talk, you know. It's good to talk," Cleo said, nodding her head. She gently placed the decoy on the floor, then walked to the books stacked up along one wall and looked at them. "Your books. This talking is like one of those good books up there. If it's good, you've got to finish it, right? Or else it's no good." She looked at him. She had his full attention, though he seemed to struggle with what she was saying. In fact, Cleo wasn't exactly sure where she was going. But she wasn't going to stop here. "Look, for some crazy reason—or maybe not so crazy—I plopped onto your island and into your world uninvited. We sailed up on that ledge in the fog, and somehow you appeared. You saved us. Maybe even from drowning. And here I am. On this island with…wow, this is crazy!" Cleo shook her head vigorously, as if shaking off a dream, her long, strawberry blond hair cascading from side to side, wrapping around and obscuring her face with each turn, until she stopped, wide-eyed. Aiden was staring at her.

"So that's why you help me?"

"No. I mean, why not? Why did *you* help us when we were stuck on that ledge?"

He didn't answer. After a long, awkward silence, Cleo turned and looked back at the crude shelves full of books. "Have you read all of these?"

"Yes."

"Where did they come from?"

"The Jesus boat."

"The Jesus boat?"

"The island missionary boat brings them for me when it comes out here to get us to pray."

"Us?"

He looked down, then took a big breath. Or maybe it was a huge sigh. Cleo couldn't tell. But it was as if he were letting go. Giving in. "It *was* us. Before," he said finally. Cleo didn't want to push things, thinking it best to take baby steps. So, she went back to the books. "I love books," she said. "I love to talk about books. What subjects are most of these? I mean, like: history, nature, mystery stories and novels?"

"All," Aiden said.

Cleo smiled. "Man, you must be the most well-read hermit in existence."

Aiden was disturbed. "I'm not a hermit. I'm with everything out here: animals, birds, fish, the sea, the moon, the tides. Everything I need."

Cleo mustered up some courage. "Except people. Look, I mean, books are great, but they're even greater when you have someone to talk to about what you've read, what you've learned. That's why, at school, it's much better because—"

"You."

"Me?"

"I have *you* to talk to now."

"Yes, but I'm just here for—"

"You brought other books. What books?"

"I brought my other summer reading book and also, well, I brought my high school yearbook."

"Why that?"

"I just thought that you might like to see all the stuff—school activities like sports, drama, dances—that regular kids get to—"

"Regular kids?"

"Well, yeah. I mean, there's nothing out here like that stuff that kids have at school."

"There are books." He frowned at her, then gave a broad, sweeping gesture at the bookshelves. "School? *This* is school."

"But there's no sharing. No one to hang out with."

"I have my people. And I have you."

Cleo put her hands on her hips. "You don't *have* me. And, for God's sake, WHAT PEOPLE?"

He didn't respond.

Cleo switched to a calm, soothing voice. "Aiden, maybe you've just been alone too long and maybe you've started to, well, imagine things. I mean, to keep you company. Which is fine, I guess. That's what my grandfather thought when I told him—"

He glared at her. "You shared all this with your grandfather?"

"Only about...only because he asked where your parents were. He was worried. Like me."

Aiden had a devastated look on his face. "You broke your promise." He sat back down on his bed.

Cleo remembered—she *had* promised. She teared up. She couldn't help it. "I'm so sorry. Really." She rubbed her arm across her wet eyes before looking at him, seeing the hurt on his face. It was like when he fell on the hill where they first met— the look of a wounded animal with nowhere to run, a wounded animal now hunched over on a homemade bed of spruce and birch branches. A wounded animal truly alone. It broke her heart.

After some moments he looked up at her. "I had thought, that finally…" But he stopped there and looked away, before slowly placing his clenched fists together over his heart and twisting them several times."

"What's that? I mean, what does that mean? Please tell me."

He didn't respond at first. Then he lowered his hands, folded them together, and placed them in his lap. "It's an ancient people's sign. The sign for grief."

"I'm so sorry, Aiden."

They sat quietly for some time, until Cleo asked, "You had started to say that you had thought, that finally…and then you stopped. You had thought that finally what?"

Without looking up, he said "That finally it would be like it once was."

"Once was? Before?"

"Before. How I felt before."

"Before? Before with your parents? With your mother?"

He held one hand over his forehead and right eye. The other eye, the emerald green one, was unfocused, as if lost somewhere back in time. "Your mother," he said finally, focused back on Cleo, "Don't you want it to be like that, too? How you felt. That feeling of being with her. Like it once was."

Her response came as sobs. The big empty hole in Cleo opened, and, hardly realizing it, she fell through. She found herself sitting on the bed next to Aiden. Then, with no forethought, she reached out to him. Held him. And as before, on the hill, she smelled that same scent of the land—the trees, resin, moss, bark, and pinecones—that still seemed to be a part of him. They held each other for what seemed a very long time. Finally, Cleo lifted her head off Aiden's shoulder, leaned back a bit, and said, "We've both been to the same place. We can trust each other now. It's safe."

"It's safe?"

"Yes, it's safe for you to tell me your story."

And so, in a slow, unmodulated voice, he told her how, in 1950, his parents James and Maggie Quinn had come to settle on the island. Reformed alcoholics, impoverished, with Maggie two months pregnant, they had been living in a homeless shelter in New Bedford, Massachusetts. They were down on their luck. Down as far as down could be. Then it all changed. They had befriended a fellow shelter resident named Matos—Aiden didn't know if that was his first or last name—who had told them of his plan to start a new life. He was going to sail his old boat to a remote Maine island he knew about, settle there, homestead, and begin a life of fishing and perhaps dairy farming. But soon after Matos had shared that, a crazed man, another resident, attacked him. James came to Matos' aid during the attack, and repelled the man. Matos was extremely grateful. A month later, when a bad health diagnosis nixed his new life plans, he gave the sailboat to James and Maggie, telling them about the location of the uninhabited island.

"Could they even sail?"

"My father knew the sea. He fished out of New Bedford for many years. Until he lost his boat."

"Oh, in a storm?"

"No. To the bank. And because of drinking."

"I'm sorry."

"But he got into AA after that. Never drank again."

Cleo thought of the courage he and Aiden's mother must have had. "They sound like good people." She looked over at Aiden. "You know, that's really brave. Taking his pregnant wife and an old boat to an unknown place, and not knowing how—"

"It was a good plan," Aiden said. "They went to work fixing up Matos' old sailboat. They just didn't give up. That's what my mom told me. They even changed the boat's name to reflect that."

"*Perseverance.*"

"You saw her in the harbor, then."

Cleo nodded. "And that's okay? I mean, changing a boat's name? My grandfather says it's bad luck to do that."

Aiden looked hard at Cleo. Said nothing. That made her uncomfortable. She looked away. Looked around the cabin. "But the winter! What about the winter out here? And on the boat!"

Aiden looked bewildered. "Winter? Winter is no problem. There are different priorities then. To survive, for one thing." He paused, a serene look coming to his face. "And it all changes, just as it does in all the seasons; the landscape changes, the wildlife, the sky, all the sounds, the look on the breaking seas. It's all a wonder."

Cleo hugged herself. "But it's COLD!"

"*Perseverance* has a woodstove, and there is plenty of wood and also a well on the island. Until my parents rebuilt the old stone cabin by the wharf, we lived aboard the boat all year. I built this cabin myself a couple years ago; it's kind of my place to read and think. Anyway, we made do. My father had a deal to use an old lobster boat for his fishing while paying for it with money from his catch." Aiden paused, seemingly lost in thought, then resumed. "We were going to try swordfishing together, heading way out, over a hundred miles, to the Northeast Canyons. Dangerous. But plenty of money in a sword. I could buy a lot of supplies for the winter with what one would bring in the market. I'm thinking of trying it alone now that he's—."

"What? What happened? Something happened to him? To them?"

Aiden didn't answer.

Cleo thought it best to move on. "So, were you born in the wintertime?" She half smiled. "God, I hope not."

"December."

"Wow! So, that's why you couldn't go ashore to be born."

"There was no money for that. Besides, were there hospitals four thousand years ago? That never stopped any of nature's creatures from being born, including humans—even right here on the island. Four thousand years ago, right here on this island were—" Aiden stopped himself suddenly.

Cleo was bold. She finished his sentence: "…the Red Paint People." He stared at her. Cleo stared back. "Remember. We share," she said.

Aiden appeared extremely nervous. "No. I can't," he said finally.

"Why? Who says you can't? Who says you can't talk? Look, it's fine to talk about people who once lived here but are gone now. My grandfather says that's how we learn—from the past."

Aiden changed the subject. "Your other books. Show me your other books. That yearbook one. I have never seen a yearbook." It appeared to Cleo that he was distracting himself—or her—from something, but she reached into her knapsack and pulled out her yearbook, opening the cover in front of him. Inside was a double page color spread of a high school football stadium, the camera focused on hundreds of students seated, standing, and cheering in the stands. Cheerleaders holding large white pom poms appeared to be dancing on the field in front of the crowd. Aiden stared at the photo, mystified. "All those people. Why do they gather? And what do the white feathers mean?"

"It's a pep rally. Before a game. Those are the pom pom girls."

Aiden looked confused. "I don't understand a pep rally, or what kind of game, or what the white feathers are for."

"The white feathers are pom poms that you shake when cheering; it's a pep rally before a big football game. The pep rally is when you try to drum up excitement to win."

He looked at her, baffled. "Why? Why win? Why not play?"

God, Cleo thought. 'Why, why'. It's like talking to my three year old nephew. Then she caught herself, realizing he really had little connection to the mainland world.

"Show me more pages," he said.

She opened it to the section of small, individual student pictures, twenty to a page. Aiden leaned closer. "You are there? Show me you."

Cleo turned a few pages until she got to her page. "It's on this page. Find me."

He found her at once, and gently placed his forefinger on her picture. He kept his finger there, leaning down, looking intently at her face. He began to stroke the small black and white photo from top to bottom, as if trying to slide her off the page and into his world. His finger finally stopped on the white string of beads around her neck. "You have beads," he said. Then, with his other hand, he fingered the beads on the cord around his neck. "I have beads."

Cleo nodded, then ventured what she knew could be a risky question. "Mine came from a store. Yours? Where did yours come from?"

Aiden reached up and fingered the beads again. "From my mother," he said.

"That's so nice. They're beautiful."

He looked at her. "You don't wear yours now?"

"No, they were for the picture."

"Only for one picture?"

"Well, I wore them a couple times after. To a dance and stuff."

He looked down at the yearbook. "A dance? Is there a dance picture in here? With you wearing a gown?" Then he glanced at his book-filled shelves. "Like when Kitty goes to the ball?"

"Huh?"

"In Tolstoy's *Anna Karenina*."

Cleo looked at him, wide-eyed. "You *read* Tolstoy?" But she saw Aiden was engrossed again, paging through the yearbook. "Actually, there *is* a dance picture," she continued. "Well, sort of. It's taken at the prom queen ball, of the queen and her court."

He looked up. "You have a queen? Show me the picture."

Cleo flipped through more pages. "Here."

Aiden leaned in. Looked wide eyed at the photo. "It's you! You are the queen?"

Cleo blushed. "Having a prom queen is something lots of schools do. The queen is a girl kids elect, a girl they choose."

He gave Cleo a questioning look. "How do they choose?"

Cleo thought for a while. "Well, the one they pick is usually someone who is nice, kind, interesting, does a lot of activities, and, I guess, pretty."

He looked up again at his shelves of books. "In my books on history, I've read much of queens and how they rule. So that girl rules the school?"

Cleo laughed. This is so weird, she thought. Like Tarzan and Jane. But she answered clearly. "God, no." But then she thought, well, sort of.

Aiden was suddenly buoyant. He smiled at her; his strangely colored eyes brightened. For the first time, it was a big smile, captivating, joyous, as if something wonderful had just been reaffirmed. He leaned forward on his cane, pulled himself up with seemingly little effort, and bowed at her. "YOU ARE THE QUEEN!" Cleo threw her head back and laughed. Aiden reached out for the yearbook, then sat down again next to her, slowly turning the pages.

After some time watching him, Cleo took a deep breath. "You know, maybe it would be good if you went to the mainland, if *you* went to school?"

He looked up at her, suddenly serious. "It will not be."

"Why not? I can tell you're smart. Heck, you've already read more than most college kids. It's clear you love to learn."

Aiden was silent for some time. Cleo decided to change course. "Did your mother fish with your dad?"

"We all fished."

"Oh. So, you went to the mainland to sell your catch? Or did people come here to buy it?"

"Both."

"So, you got to go to the mainland?"

"My parents didn't want me to, but when I was bigger and stronger, they wanted me there to unload."

"Why didn't they want you to go to the mainland?" He looked at her, as if being cross-examined. "Sorry, just curious," Cleo said.

But he continued. "It was not part of the life we wanted. The mainland was the life my parents left behind. A place which had given them pain. They built their own new world. Out here! A way to live the way they wanted. They made a place here. And then they taught me everything: fishing, hunting, foraging, cooking, woodworking, and reading. We all read. Always. It was our way of bringing the outside world in without any danger. All of it was enough. It was more than enough."

"But a life without people?"

"How many people does a life need?"

"Okay. But what about when people come to you, just come out here? Summer people. Developers. Sailors. Like us."

"When they come, we make it unpleasant. Unwelcome."

Cleo smirked. "I can see that. Because it almost worked with us. It almost worked with me!" Then she raised her arms with her palms up, lifted her chin in a regal manner, and stood. "But it couldn't work, could it?"

"Why?"

"Because *I* am a queen!"

Aiden laughed. It was another first. Cleo grabbed the opportunity to slide in another question. "So how *do* you make visitors feel unwelcome about coming on the island?"

"Poison."

"What? Poison?"

"Stinging Nettle, Poison Sumac, Poison Oak, Poison Ivy, Giant Hogweed. My dad would post signs with all of this and a skull and crossbones."

"Oh my God." Cleo looked down at her bare ankles. "You have these things here."

Aiden smiled. Shook his head.

Cleo smiled back. "Ah, got it! But it keeps the developers away, right? You know, you should throw ghosts into that mix. That would do it for sure."

Aiden's mood changed suddenly. He shook his head and looked toward the door of the cabin, fixated once again on something, and nodding. Cleo got nervous again; maybe it really wasn't safe here with him. "Look, I think you're all set. I should go." Aiden reached out and grabbed her arm. She looked at him, alarmed. "Let me go. Hey! You need to let go of me!"

But he held on, a look of anguish on his face. "You need to understand. Please. Please."

"Understand what? Look, first you need to let me go. RIGHT NOW!"

He let go at once and looked at her deeply, nervously fingering the beads around his neck. "I'm sorry. Bad people came once, and then I—"

Cleo took a step back, unsure of her next move. "Bad people?"

Aiden nodded. Said nothing. Then it struck Cleo: it was that writing in the journal on his table—she remembered two lines:

My prey that held her screaming in rough hands
Held the one who mated once for me,

She looked at his face, now a mixture of grief and agony. Cleo took a breath and another small step back, scared how he might react to her next statement. "I read your journal. About an osprey and something horrible sounding. Sorry, but it was there, open, on the table. For God's sake, what happened? How can I help?"

"You said we share. You said that it's safe if we share. That I have your trust. That you will tell no one."

"Yes."

He lifted his head back, looked at the ceiling, took a deep breath, closed his eyes, and spoke as if reciting from memory. "I was a young boy. Seven. It was summer. It was back when we were all living part of the time on the boat and part of it in the old stone house down by the wharf. My father went to the mainland to get a part for the motor of our fishing boat. He took the small outboard skiff. And when he got to Jonesport he then had to travel by bus all the way to Portland that next day and then the part wasn't there. So, he waited there, sleeping on a fisherman friend's boat at the wharf in Portland that night. My mother and I were alone on the island for two nights. On the second night while we were sleeping two men came ashore." Aiden shook his head, as if trying to will something bad away, as if to shake off a dream. "They came into the cabin. Woke us. Stumbled around. There was drink on their breath. One of them grabbed me. Carried me outside, behind the cabin. Held me there. Then I heard the screams from my mother. Inside the cabin. They seemed to go on forever. Finally, the man who held me brought me back by the door, and handed me to the other one who came out. And that one brought me back behind the cabin. Held me down again. Told me he would kill me if I ever said anything. My mother screamed again. And again. I tried to pull away. I tried with everything in me."

Cleo felt paralyzed. She put her hands to her face. Aiden looked at her. He waited to speak until she dropped her hands and looked at him. "*They* are the prey," he said.

Cleo wasn't sure if this was real or imagined. She flashed on the story Poppy had told her about the two women murdered on the Isles of Shoals. Had Aiden heard this story? If so, did his mind take that story and...

Not knowing what else to say, Cleo asked, "The police? Or did your mom tell your dad so that he could—"

Aiden shook his head. "No. My mother made me promise never to tell my father. She feared he would track down the two and kill them, and that would make our lives change forever. There would be no island home anymore and he would be in jail." He looked at her. "So, I kept my promise."

"My God. That must have been so hard."

Aiden nodded slowly. He was silent for some time. Lost in thought. Finally, he said, "When I was little, after it happened, I just didn't know what to say to her." He looked at Cleo, wide eyed, his voice pleading. "How can a little boy see something like that and know what to do, what to say? How? I barely knew what it *was*. I barely understood what was happening. Only that they hurt her. That she screamed. And screamed. And that after that night she was different. So how would I know what to say to her? How could I know how to help her make that pain go away, that pain that I saw in her eyes ever after? That pain was *in* her. I could see it. And I knew what it looked like because it is in me too. It follows me; it follows me at sea, in my sleep, out on the cliff when I look out to sea. How do I shake it? How do you shake a ghost when …" His voice trailed off.

Cleo wanted to tell him of her own pain, thinking that might help, but before she could say anything, Aiden continued. "You know, she read to me all the time when I was little. That's what got me so into reading. And the summer when they did this to her, she had been reading to me from the third book of *The Chronicles of Narnia*. Have you read it?"

Cleo shook her head. "I should have, I guess. Every other kid seems to have."

"Narnia is this fantasy world of magic, mythical beasts, and talking animals. So these children from the real world are transported to Narnia. After the evil happened to her, when my mom read that book to me, I desperately wanted to join those children, to go there, to help them protect Narnia from evil. It was the only thing I could think of doing after what happened." His voice cracked. "The only way I thought I could make things better."

"Those two men, the ones who—"

Aiden raised his hand. Stopped her. Held up his left hand, palm facing him. "When she read to me, she always held the book out in her left hand and put her other arm around my shoulder, like keeping us both together inside the book. Sometimes she'd stroke my hair with her fingers while reading and then, when it was time to turn the page, she'd just reach down with that arm that was around my little shoulder and turn the page in front of me, and then when the page turned things changed." He was quiet for a while. He began to sob. "So see? That's what *I* wanted to do! With what had happened to her. Just turn the page. Make things change. But I didn't know how. It wasn't a book. It was real."

Amidst tears of her own now, Cleo thoughts went to her own mother, of how they had sat together, how she had read to her. And how she had slowly dwindled away.

Aiden continued. "Even when I was much older, fifteen or so, I could still see the hurt in her…see her suddenly sob for what seemed like no reason. But I knew the reason. I knew what was locked inside her."

Cleo spoke. Adamant now. "Aiden, you *need* to talk to someone about this."

He looked at her as if what she said was the most obvious thing in the world. "I am," he said. "I'm talking to you."

"You know what I mean. A professional."

"No. We will get revenge. And that may scare the ghosts away as well. It is almost done." Aiden looked to the side of the room. Nodded at the empty wall. "They are helping."

Cleo looked at him, sternly now. It surprised her, but her bravado was suddenly back. "The tribe? Aiden, there is no tribe."

He reached under the bed, pulled out the slate bayonet, and held it up in front of her. "This! This belongs to the tribe."

Cleo took another deep breath. "Aiden, I think you need to talk to someone about all this: your mom's assault, this tribe you see, your missing parents. Go to the mainland. Talk to someone who knows how to deal with this."

He looked at her questioningly. "What kind of person is that?"

Cleo took a deep breath. "Maybe a doctor."

"I am not sick. I am strong. Healthy."

"You're seeing things that are not there. Aiden, why can't I see the tribe? Answer me that."

"You question me? That this is not real?" He lifted the bayonet higher. Shook it. Can you see this? Is this here? Does this exist?"

Cleo nodded.

"Then where did this come from?"

"I guess from a tribe, maybe from those hunter gatherer people. But many years ago. Not now!" He didn't respond.

Aiden put the bayonet down gently, slid it under the bed.

"Aiden, I can help by getting you help."

He smirked at her. "What? With your 'professional'?"

"Look, you've been out here alone too long. You need somebody. I mean, didn't you feel even a little better by sharing this horrible thing with me? Won't more of that help? Help you heal?"

"Heal? How do I heal from that?"

Cleo thought for a while, flashed on things in her own life that needed healing. Finally, she said, "I just don't think revenge is the answer."

Aiden pointed to the door of the cabin. His look was stark. "Then you should go."

Cleo reached down and picked up her knapsack, pulled it open, pulled out some cans of food, and placed them on the table. She headed for the door, but then she had a thought. She reached back into her knapsack, and pulled out *Siddhartha*. She handed him the book. "Keep it. I'm done with my summer reading. Maybe you'll find the answer in here," she said, and headed for the door.

"Stop!" He held up the book. "Why this book?"

Cleo was frustrated. "Read it and find out."

"Tell me what I will find out. Please."

"You need to share more. Okay?"

Aiden closed his eyes for a few moments. "What do you want to know?"

"Well, for one: where are your parents now?" He gave no response. "God, how hard is that to answer?"

He opened his eyes. "Very hard to answer," he said, finally.

Cleo stood still. Confused. "Well, when did you last see them?"

Aiden took a deep breath. "285 days ago. They were headed out to pull our nets, out by Whaleback."

"285 days ago! Whaleback?"

"Whaleback Ledge. They never returned."

"Oh my God! Did you call the Coast Guard? Look for them? I mean—"

"I looked for them. I have looked for them all these days." He glanced at his ankle. "I will look again when this foot heals."

"Now there's no chance...is there? After so long." Cleo paused. "Shouldn't you have called someone else to search, too? I mean, right away. Earlier."

"The authorities would take me away if they knew I had no parents. I am still a minor. They would bring me to the mainland if they knew I was out here alone. Make me live there. Go to school. I would never fit in there. I know that. I feel it when I go ashore to sell my catch and buy supplies."

"Why?"

"Because people stare at me." Aiden stopped. Shook his head.

"Stare at you?"

"Yes. Last week was the worst. I usually go in very early when there aren't many people about, but this time I went in later in the day. In the afternoon. Big mistake. Plus, it was really hot. I went to Mugford's Grocery and got a few things. That went okay. Then to Crowley Hardware. Old man Crowley asked how things were out on the island; he said it was odd that he hadn't seen my folks lately. He asked if they were okay. That made me nervous. I just nodded. Anyway, walking back to the boat in that heat got me to thinking about ice cream, so I changed course to this place called Lisa's Snack Shack, where I knew they had some. I got one of those vanilla chocolate swirl cones and sat at a picnic table under one of the awnings they had around the side of the store. Right then a couple cars pulled up and a bunch of kids about my age got out and lined up by the ice cream window. They got their cones and came around by me and sat at a big table under the other awning, laughing and joking and carrying on. I was facing them because of the way I was situated on the bench, so I just looked down at my ice cream and minded my own business. Once in a while I snuck a look, though. I could see one of the girls doing the same to me. Then the boy next to her sees her doing that and he starts looking at me. Then he starts looking over at the girl, looking mad. I figured it was time to go. So I got up, half my cone still in my hand, and headed out. But the only way around the shack was close to their table, so I just licked my cone and looked ahead. I almost made it past. Until the guy next to the girl said, "Hey Tarzan. You better save some of that ice cream for your ape family on the island."

Cleo's eyes widened. "That's sick. Oh my God, what did you do?"

"I had read about Tarzan. So I said, 'You must be mistaken. My name is Aiden, not Tarzan. Tarzan was the creation of a man named Edgar Burroughs, inspired by the story of a young English nobleman who was shipwrecked off the African Coast in the nineteenth century.'"

"Then what happened?"

"Well, it got really quiet. And I just walked away."

Cleo smiled. Raised a fist in the air. "Perfect!"

"Perfect?"

"Yeah. You know, if you'd just smiled back and taken that taunt of his, he'd have won.

But you *totally* put him down!"

"Maybe. I don't know. Maybe the real Tarzan wouldn't have taken any shit."

"Ha! And done what? Grabbed the nearest vine and swung into the table and knocked them all over like a bunch of bowling pins?"

Aiden looked down. "I know what they think about me. They think I'm strange. Illiterate. They don't know what I know. How much I've read and learned and thought about. They don't know what is on this island…about the ancient people, the tribe. How rich in life it is. No. I will never go ashore to live. This is my island. I was born here. This has always been my home."

"But Aiden, you could really give back if you were with people. You're smart. You're an artist. Those decoys! And that Osprey poem; it just froze me. You can *really* write. You're athletic. I saw you throw that spear. And you know so much about nature, about the natural world. All this. All this! People would look up to you!"

"Look up to me? People *stare* at me!"

Cleo shook her head. "Well, maybe that's because you're also pretty damned good to look at, too."

There was a long silence. Aiden seemed calmer. He spoke, and for the first time he used her name: "Cleo, can't you understand that this is where I belong. Does anyone have the right to say where I should be? What right does anyone have to say where anyone should be."

Cleo couldn't comprehend what being alone for 285 days would be like. Or why anyone would want that. Or what would happen to one's mind. Then it dawned on her—*he thinks he's not alone. He made company for himself. To survive all this incredible loss.* She had an idea. She took a deep breath, and spoke almost casually. "So…when did you first meet this tribe?"

Aiden looked at Cleo skeptically. "When?"

"Yes. Was it before your parents disappeared?"

"No. After. It was during bird migration season. April."

"Four or five months ago? And the tribe came out here?"

"No. They were always here."

Cleo looked under his bed and gestured at the bayonet. "Did they give you that?"

"No. It was buried with some of the others. Under the red powder."

"You dug this up?"

"Yes. The others told me to keep it."

"Oh. And that spear I saw you throwing. They gave you that?"

"No. I made that. I have books on ancient people, tools, and weapons."

Cleo began to think that maybe the approach she was taking was wrong. Maybe she was enabling him. "So…without your parents you don't mind being alone now?"

"I am still not alone. I live with the birds, fish, wildlife, vegetation, the tribe."

"Yes, but—"

"Have you ever talked to animals? That is how it should be. If you get to know them, they are the best of company." He went on to tell her of the birds he listened to and even spoke to during different seasons and migrations while growing up, the many species that would rest and feed on the island during their long northbound trip. "And the warblers. Warblers are everywhere on Gadus," he said with awe, pride, and a sense of stewardship in his voice, as if the birds were all his charge on his island. He told her of the yellow warblers' series of six to ten whistled notes, sounding like *sweet, sweet, sweet, I'm so sweet.* And he described other songbirds such as scarlet tanagers, thrushes, flycatchers, white-throated sparrow, and the year-round residents such as chickadees, nuthatches, tufted titmouse, and several woodpecker species. Then he looked at her with a nodding gesture. "Being such a good, capable creature as you say I am—a nature lover, artist, writer, athlete, and even good to look at—you should want to be here with such a person."

Cleo stepped back. This was becoming all too much again. Yet he needed help. Badly. She couldn't just leave now, sail away with Poppy, leaving him out here without… Her mind was racing.

Aiden interrupted her thoughts. "You'll share now? About this book you brought."

Cleo paused, thinking strategically. "See, you really like to talk about books. Imagine doing that with others. Doing that with lots of others! Or writing books for others. About all you've learned out here. Your amazing story."

"I would never do that. And, besides, I can talk of books with you."

"But don't you want to hang out with other people? Make good friends?" Cleo took a breath. "Maybe love someone?"

"I have loved others. And they disappeared. He held up *Siddhartha*. "Tell me about it."

"Okay. Well, I guess it's about finding enlightenment and love. It's about this boy Siddhartha, a Brahmin son—"

"Wait. What is Brahmin?"

"It's a high ranking social class in India. Anyway, this boy Siddhartha isn't able to find enlightenment and his place in the world, so he goes on this long search for that, and the book follows him on this quest."

"Does he find it?"

"Yes."

"How?"

"By listening to the river," Cleo said. She watched Aiden's reaction, certain there would be a cocked head and a follow-up question. Instead, she saw him nod as if truly understanding. "Wait, you get it?"

"Yes."

"I mean, it took me the whole book to…and still… really? … you get it? So, what does the river say?"

"That we *are* the river. Just as we are one with the tides and the sea. As we are one with the sky and the clouds. I am that here. On this island. One. So, as I told you, there is no reason for me to leave this island, not for enlightenment or people, or anything else."

Cleo nodded; she was half convinced Aiden was right. And she was convinced he was very smart. She relaxed a bit. "God, I wish I could get you to write my paper on this. And you didn't even read the book yet!" She put her forefinger to her lips. "Hmmm, maybe I should bring *you* back to class." She looked at him and smiled. "I know, I know. That won't happen."

Aiden opened the book to a bookmarked page with the top corner turned down. He began reading, concentrating intently, mouthing the words as he read. Cleo knew what page he was on. *She drew him toward her with her eyes, he inclined his face toward hers and laid his mouth on her mouth, which was like a freshly split-open fig. For a long time, he kissed Kamala, and Siddhartha was filled with deep astonishment ...*

Aiden looked up at Cleo. "Why do you save this page? Who is Kamala?"

Cleo flushed. Looked down. Finally, she said, "I saved it because it, well, it seemed heavy."

"Heavy?"

Cleo moved away, began to pace, hands over her head, pulling back on her long hair.

"What is wrong?"

"God, this is all so weird."

"What is weird? Tell me."

"I can't explain why. It just feels that way. With Kamala and Siddhartha, it's just, when he was on his journey, they were lovers, okay? Kamala tries to help him stop from emptying himself of all his joy and dreams, which was what he thought he had to do to find enlightenment. She helps him just be what he is right now. Like the river, I guess. To let it flow. Leave it be. He remembers he can write poetry, and he creates a poem on the spot for Kamala, about how sacrificing to her is lovelier than sacrificing to the gods. Kamala is impressed and agrees to give Siddhartha a kiss for his skill. And I felt—"

Aiden stared down at the page. Said nothing.

"Look, I don't know what I'm thinking. Maybe you should just read the book to find out," Cleo said.

He looked up at her. Concern filled his face. She stopped pacing, moved a bit closer to him. Aiden's brow was furrowed. He looked very concerned. "Does he lose her? Does Siddhartha lose her? Tell me."

Cleo nodded. "Much later. She dies of a snakebite, but just before she—". Cleo stopped there.

"Just before she what?"

"Just before she dies, she tells him that he is the father of their child."

Aiden smiled. "So, there's a little Siddhartha? To keep things going. That would be good."

Cleo smiled. "Yes," she said. "And speaking of going, I should really be going, too. My grandfather is—"

Aiden stood, this time without the help of his cane. Then he bowed at her. Cleo smiled again, tilted her head, gave him a questioning look. "What's with the bowing? Like you're bowing goodbye?"

"No goodbye."

"What then?"

"I would like to dance with the queen."

Cleo laughed. She felt pulled in two directions: part of her did want to dance, yet she feared what might come of it. "Your foot, though? I don't think you can dance on it. And do you even know how to dance?"

"No. But I have read of it." There was a sincere, eager look in his eyes. "You can teach me," he continued. "Teach me. Please."

Cleo wanted to give herself more maneuver room, or perhaps more escape room. "Outside, then. In the fresh air. We can dance in the soft grass," she said. "It will be easier on your foot. But use your cane." She handed it to him, then held the screen door as he made his way outside. The sun, high now, sent sporadic bolts of light through the waving pine branches, illuminating the grasses in varying spots. They moved slowly along toward the hilly point where Aiden said they would find a good dancing spot with a view. Cleo winced with each of Aiden's steps, thinking of the pain in his ankle although, being behind him, she couldn't see his face. Perhaps it doesn't hurt anymore, she thought as they moved along. She began to hear the sound of surf, then saw a clearing ahead, and then a semi-circular cove with a stone-filled beach below. They walked through patches of tall grass. Many were pressed down, mixing with an inviting, mossy ground cover. "It's as if deer or some other animals have come here to sleep," Cleo said.

Aiden turned. "Yes," he said. "Deer and also myself. To rest, and to think. And to just look." He bent down and pulled up a flowering plant. He handed it to her.

"It's beautiful," Cleo said, looking closely at the lustrous leaves and profusion of small, deep pink, saucer-shaped flowers.

"It's sheep laurel," Aiden said. "I have a book on flowers. It's one of my favorites. It's poisonous to people, but attracts lots of pollinators—bees and butterflies." He stopped and looked at her. "Maybe that's because it's so beautiful." He gazed down at the flower again. "I love to watch the bees dance from flower to flower; the way they land so lightly is mesmerizing. Like a dance. He leaned down, pointing into one of the flowers. "Do you know the reproductive parts?" he asked in an innocent, natural way.

Cleo flushed. "No, I really hadn't thought about that…with flowers, I mean."

"The pistil and the stigma. The stigma is the receptive base on which the pollen lands. Look closely." She held the flower still. Aiden leaned closer to her, pointing to the inner parts of one of the flowers. Just then, as if on cue, a bee landed on the flower in Cleo's hand. She jerked her head back. "Don't worry. It's safe. That's a solitary bee. They're not aggressive," he said.

"But still, even if it's just one—"

"No, I mean, that's a kind of bee by name, called a Solitary. Different from honeybees and bumblebees. They live alone, not in hives. And they don't produce honey." He looked at Cleo and smiled. "And they don't have a queen." Aiden looked back down at the bee and pointed. "Look! She's placed her feet in a groove that contains the flower's pollen sacs." He was clearly entranced. "Can you see? This is a wonder of nature." He looked at Cleo again. "Do you now see all that's out here on this island? Do you see how much we have?"

"Sure. I mean, it's wonderful. There are lots of cool things. But they're not just out here, on this island, Aiden."

"But here is where we are. Here is now. Right? Like the river. Like that Siddhartha."

Cleo stepped back, then handed him the branch with the flowers. She smiled and pointed in the direction of the path leading back to the harbor and *Archaic*. "And *there* is where I need to go now: back to the boat with my grandfather. I've been gone too long."

Aiden lowered his eyes. "So, does this mean I will never dance with a queen."

Cleo smiled again. "You're too much! Okay. But just the box step."

"What is that?"

Cleo thought for a moment. "It's kind of a waltz."

Aiden dropped his cane, and carefully laid down the flower branch. He bowed again. Cleo smiled and faced him, standing straight.

"Now," she said, "you should follow the queen's lead this first time since it's new to you. Usually, the boy leads, but I'll lead you along this time to make it flow. Think of the box step like drawing a box on the ground with your feet. That's how I learned it. Of course, it's better to have music! Oh, well. Ready? So, stand straight, put your feet together with your weight on your right foot. Careful of the foot, though. Now lift your left arm to the height of my shoulder and take my right hand." Cleo reached out. Aiden followed. "Now take your right arm and wrap it around my back and place your hand between my shoulder blades." Aiden followed. "Good. But does your bad ankle feel okay?" Aiden nodded, and Cleo completed her instructions. "So, here we go again, and I'll do a beat, so it's almost like music: one-two-three, one-two-three, one-two-three…" And off they went, dancing face-to-face, moving awkwardly through the tall grass in the clearing by the sea. Positioned as they were, it was hard to avert each other's eyes, and this made Cleo self-conscious. She tried to look away, but Aiden's stare held her to him. She felt the heat of his hand pressed between her bare shoulder blades. A trickle of sweat slid down her back and beneath the light cloth of her tank top. After some time, Aiden stopped dancing, but still held her, pulling her close, his chin now over her shoulder, his mouth close to her ear. They stayed still like that for a while. Then he spoke softly, prayerlike, almost in a whisper: "You are a force in the nature I love, the ocean below, and the sky above." He pulled his head back. Looked at her. "That's my poem. Like Siddhartha." Cleo began to sob, though she wasn't sure why. Maybe it was about loss, maybe about innocence, or maybe confusion about

123

being caught in the web of his nature. She thought of the solitary bee hovering over the deep pink flower that Aiden loved. It was all so right. And impossible. She lifted her head from Aiden's shoulder, looked up at him, ready to say she was touched by his poem, but it just couldn't work between them. Instead, before she could speak, he did as Siddhartha had done, inclining his face toward hers, laying his mouth on her mouth. Cleo's thoughts fell away. Her world spun. For how long she would never be sure, until somehow, she was down in the long grass with him, kissing still. After some time, he pulled away a bit, just enough to focus on her face, and then he looked down at her breasts. "I can touch you there?" he asked. Cleo took a deep breath and smiled. "You don't ask that," she said. He looked confused. "You just try it, silly, and then the girl decides whether to let you or not." And so, he tried. And the girl let him, and then she let his hands roam free while they kissed for what seemed forever. And when the shafts of light that pierced the spruce branches disappeared with the declining sun, and they lay in shadow, he asked again for something more. And by then the girl was beyond deciding. She just was.

* * *

Halfway down the path in front of the cabin, on her way back to the boat, Cleo turned and looked back. Aiden stood in the door, leaning against one side for support. She waved.

"Please come back," he said. "I have something to give you."

She came back to the door. Aiden held out his closed hand. "This was my mother's," he said. When he opened his hand, it held a colorful, small, smooth, oblong stone figurine, a pendant with a hole in the top. "I found it here and gave it to my mom for her birthday a couple years ago. It's a heliotrope gemstone; they're ancient symbols for eternal love, prophetic dreams, courage, and healing." He looked away, seaward. "I told her to wear it always. But the day she disappeared I found it in the cabin. The cord had broken, so she must have left it behind that day when she went out fishing with my father." He looked back at Cleo. "I want you to have it, to wear it, so we are one in eternal love."

Cleo was reticent. "But it's your mother's. I wouldn't feel—"

"Don't you want eternal love?"

Cleo took the pendant from his hand. "You'll want to get a stronger cord. I tied it back together, though. Perhaps get a chain," he said.

"Thank you. I'll treasure this. Always." Cleo slid it over her head.

Aiden nodded, encouraged. "And I will write another poem for you. A longer one. A better one. When you return, you will see," he said.

Cleo wiped her eyes. "Aiden, we went through this a hundred times. I *have* to go. I can't stay on this island. My first year in college starts in two weeks."

"But now is now. Right now. You said that. Siddhartha said that."

"I told you, come with us. Let us take you ashore. My grandfather is very wise, and he knows a lot of people who can help you. And then we can still see each other. It's perfect."

"No. I have more to do."

Cleo shook her head. "We talked about this too, Aiden. Those two men. They're not coming back out here. But you can try to bring them to justice in another way. From being ashore. By being on the mainland. With the help of the law."

He smirked. "And who will believe the word of a crazy island boy about something that no one else saw, something that happened ten years ago? A crazy island boy whose parents have now mysteriously disappeared."

"Please, Aiden. Can you just think about it? Tonight? Think about it tonight. Look, I tell you what: I can come back first thing in the morning if you *promise* me now that you'll think about it, and then we can make plans. Okay? Okay? Please?"

"Come back in the morning, then."

Cleo smiled. It felt like a victory. Maybe she could have it all, she thought: be his rescuer, help right a wrong, and be his...." But she curtailed that thought. "Cool," she said, finally. "This is good. This is best." She blew Aiden a kiss, and headed back down the path. Just as the trail began to descend, she heard him speak. She turned again. "What? I didn't hear."

"There's only one now," he said.

"I know. I know. Now is now. *Siddhartha.*" She smiled. "But later is better than now this time."

"No, I don't mean that."

"What?"

"One of the two, only one is left now."

Cleo froze. Her face prickled. She moved a few steps closer to the cabin.

Aiden said nothing, a solemn look on his face.

"Maybe I shouldn't ask, but where's the one who *isn't* left?"

He nodded. A look of satisfaction in his eyes. "He's where he should be."

Cleo backed away. Turned to leave.

"I will think tonight," he called. "And then I will see you in the morning. As you promised. As we keep all our promises."

* * *

Cleo looked west as she descended along the trail to the wharf. She didn't have a watch, but knew it was way past the time when she should have returned. The sun was getting low, and the air was cooling. Cleo was cooling as well; the profundity of all that had transpired replaced the flush of romance that first filled her. Aiden's last words echoed in her mind as she jogged along: ...*we keep all our promises... we keep all our promises...* What to do? She was becoming frantic about what, if anything, she should tell Poppy. And what would she do after hearing Aiden's decision, whatever it was, when she returned in the morning.

When she got within sight of the wharf, she was relieved to see that Poppy was still ashore, but his pacing back and forth by the wharf ladder concerned her. She was surprised he seemed as anxious as she was. As she approached the wharf edge, she saw that his tools were already in their skiff below. "Is everything okay, Poppy?"

"Glad you're back. I would have tried to find you, but was afraid we'd cross each other unseen somehow, and then you'd show up here and find me gone. Anyway, weather's coming in. Coming in bad. And soon. My weather receiver is calling for a three day blow. We're vulnerable in this harbor because of the wind direction that's coming. But we still have two or three hours of daylight, so we'll be heading out right away to grab a safe harbor to the west. Also, Cleo, we can't afford to lose any more time, or you won't make it back for college orientation."

Cleo knew she had no choice. It wasn't even worth bringing up her plan for the next morning. They headed down the ladder, rowed out to *Archaic*, climbed aboard, and began to stow their gear before heading out. "We'll run the motor, but we'll also raise the main and staysail in case we lose power. I still don't trust this engine, especially around all those outer ledges. There should be enough wind to sail clear of the ledges if we have to default to sail power," Poppy said.

After a few moments he turned to Cleo, who hadn't responded. She was staring at the island. "Hey, Ohkuk, snap out of it. We need to go." Together they raised the sails. Then Poppy started the old gas engine and moved *Archaic* slowly forward as Cleo winched in the anchor. Once they had cleared the harbor entrance and rounded the hilly point of land, Poppy turned to look at the island. "Sorry we came up nearly empty on artifacts, my dear. But I'm glad we did this. Glad we had this last chance to look, given what's supposed to happen here next year."

Cleo turned to him. "Next year? What? What happens?"

"I guess I never mentioned it. Conservation Land Trust is taking over. Caring for the island. That's what I read, anyway. I guess the island's owners—three brothers—fought over what to do with it. Had it tied up in court all these years. One wanted to sell it, one wanted to develop it, and the other wanted to donate it to a non-profit for tax purposes." He shook his head. "I'd love to know the details of how that finally got resolved." He turned to his granddaughter before continuing. "You'd think—"

But then he saw that Cleo was transfixed. Poppy followed her stare. A lone, still figure was standing on the hill by the tower. "Well, will you look at that!" Poppy said. "Someone's saying goodbye. Huh. Either his ankle is better, or he hobbled all that way!" They were too far away to make out the expression on Aiden's face, but Cleo knew what it must have been.

"They'll need a caretaker," Poppy continued. "That young man would be perfect. A built-in caretaker." Cleo didn't respond, but continued to stare at the solitary shrinking figure. Poppy looked at his granddaughter. "Are you okay? You look almost seasick. But you never—"

"And who cares for the caretaker?" Cleo said, more to herself than to her grandfather.

Poppy didn't respond. Instead, he looked west, toward the mainland, in hopes of reaching safe harbor before the storm.

VIII

July 9, 1985 – Afternoon
Leaving Gadus Island

When Cleo returned to the wharf, she found Sophie sitting on the top of a half broken, weathered red picnic table next to two blue plastic bait barrels. Her knees were tucked under her chin. She looked up at her mother. Cleo couldn't tell if she was glad to see her.

"That took a long time," Sophie said finally. "Did you find whatever you were looking for?"

Cleo looked out at the small harbor. "Fog's finally lifting," she said. "Don't you think we should head out? Get you home to the life you want."

Sophie slid off the tabletop. Dusted off her rear end. Gave her mother a slight smile. "I thought you'd never ask."

"Well, as long as *Archaic*'s engine fires up, we're on our way," Cleo said, as they headed for the wharf ladder and out to the boat.

An hour later, as they motored out of the harbor, Cleo turned to Sophie. "By the way, I hope you didn't want to say goodbye to Cucumber Boy; it's a little late now."

Sophie shook her head. "That was never going to work, Mom."

"I didn't think you even wanted it to work."

She cocked her head, as if uncertain. "Well…"

"Oh. So, he wasn't such a nerd after all?"

Cleo was surprised she got a response; even more surprised by the response she got. "Cary was actually kinda cool," Sophie said. "Been through a lot of stuff. And knows a lot of stuff. Like, he told me some crazy things about butterflies, this whole cycle of life thing with caterpillars and butterflies. Did you know that…"

Cleo listened attentively as Sophie went on about how a beautiful monarch had landed on her arm, and what Cary had told her about the metamorphosis of butterflies. "That's so cool," Cleo said when

Sophie had finished. She stopped there, smiling thoughtfully at her daughter. She didn't want to push too hard, fearful she could fracture such a positive moment.

After a few minutes, Sophie moved to her usual spot on the cockpit bridge deck, and stared ahead, west, toward home. Cleo looked down at the old binnacle, and adjusted course a bit to starboard, keeping a close eye on the ledges to the west. She knew they were a safe distance off; still, she was anxious to get past them. From under her t-shirt, she pulled out the pendant that hung from her neck, and fingered it absently. An errant wave smacked *Archaic* just right, and a bit of spray forced Sophie to turn her head away, back toward her mother.

"Hey, where did you ever get that thing, anyway?" Sophie asked, pointing at the pendant. "It's weird. Seems like you're always wearing it." She squinted, looking skeptically at the stone.

Her mother didn't respond.

"Mom?"

Cleo took a deep breath. "Your father gave it to me."

"Huh. Well, I'm glad Dad at least gave you *something* you like."

As Sophie spoke, the roar of a large, surging ocean swell—a freak, really, much bigger than the others—rolled over the usually submerged ledge guarding the island, exposing its coal black underbelly for a few moments. Sophie looked anxiously toward the sound, but Cleo didn't turn. She knew what it was. Instead, she looked back at the empty hill and the tower on the island. Maybe she *shouldn't* tell her, she thought. Ever. Maybe it would raise too many questions. And so, she turned back and simply smiled at her daughter, who was still looking for the source of the sound. But the ledge had disappeared.

"Sophie, your father gave me the best of all things," she said finally.

Sophie turned back toward her mother. "Really, Mom? What?"

Cleo lightly stroked the stone pendant with her forefinger before tucking it back under her t-shirt. Then she looked back again at the island. "He gave me you," she said.

And somehow, for now anyway, that seemed to say enough.

# # #

Author's Note

Though this is a work of fiction, it was inspired by events that occurred over twenty years ago on an island similar to Gadus. Here is what happened:

We shouldn't have tried it, but my friend Bryan and I were both tired and desperately wanted a place to anchor, a place to sleep after an eighteen hour, overnight sail in my little twenty-five foot sloop, *Chang Ho*. As we got closer to our landfall, a small offshore island with a tiny slit of a harbor, the fog dropped on us, as if in warning not to enter. Still, we cautiously approached what we judged to be the entrance, though we had close to zero visibility, knew we were surrounded by hull-crushing ledges, and knew that the mariners' directions said to avoid the entrance at all costs in bad visibility. We missed the entrance, and almost drove my little boat onto the island's bold, rocky shore, which morphed from the curtain of fog a hundred feet dead ahead. We spun around, retreated out to sea, and headed for a safer harbor. For several years it bothered me that we hadn't made it in, and I vowed to try again, as there was something pulling at me, some intrigue, that I couldn't articulate. That next try, with my young teenaged son as crew this time, the little *Chang Ho* made it in.

It was later that afternoon when I first met the boy who inspired this story, a laconic, handsome, longhaired youth who came alongside in his skiff to sell us lobsters. After he sold them, he invited himself aboard to eat them with us, a clever move indeed. It was early that evening, down in the cabin under the glow of the paraffin lantern, that I finally got him to open up a bit, and that was only after he had decimated his newly cooked lobster, along with five or six pieces of bread. He told us he was raised since birth on this tiny island, living year round aboard a decrepit (his word) mast-less wooden sloop with his parents, eking (his word) out a living fishing. When I said, "You speak well," he looked over at his sailboat home moored behind us, and replied, "We keep the boat filled with books, books of all subjects, and I read all of them." When I asked if he missed the mainland, missed the outside world, he said no, that he would always stay on the island, that he had seldom gone ashore in his life, and most of those times didn't go so well. "I'll probably die out here," he said. There was a long pause then. I remember the silence, and the gentle swell that lifted the little *Chang Ho*, seeming to urge him on a bit. Then he stood and looked seaward, out the hatch. "Or maybe out there," he said finally.

When he did die, he was only 27 years old. And he was 'out there'. Fishing.

A note about the Red Paint People
and two special acknowledgements

A remarkable prehistoric culture, the Red Paint People flourished 4,000 years ago and lived along the coasts and rivers of New England and Atlantic Canada. Advanced for their time, they were capable of catching dangerous swordfish and crafting tools. Then the culture vanished. No one knows why. Archaeologists are hopeful that they will discover more about this ancient civilization, but for now, the Red Paint People remain shrouded in mystery.

I'm very grateful for the scholarship of Bruce Bourque, a Curator of Archaeology at the Maine State Museum and author of *The Swordfish Hunters*, and for the unwavering and passionate guidance of my close friend and amateur archeologist Bryan Burns, a man who loves the past. Any errors, omissions, inaccuracies, or wrong assumptions related to archeology and the Red Paint People are purely my own.

Made in the USA
Las Vegas, NV
20 November 2023

81218051R00090